THE
MAKING
OF A

Butterfly

A JOURNEY TO SELF-LOVE

Yolanda Bradford

Capucia LLC
211 Pauline Drive #513
York, PA 17402
www.capuciapublishing.com
Send questions to: support@capuciapublishing.com

Paperback ISBN: 978-1-954920-34-7
eBook ISBN: 978-1-954920-35-4
Library of Congress Control Number: 2022913155

Cover Design: Ranilo Cabo
Layout: Ranilo Cabo
Book Midwife: Karen Everitt

Printed in the United States of America

Capucia LLC is proud to be a part of the Tree Neutral® program. Tree Neutral offsets the number of trees consumed in the production and printing of this book by taking proactive steps such as planting trees in direct proportion to the number of trees used to print books. To learn more about Tree Neutral, please visit treeneutral.com.

To my loving Grandmother, Ernestine Cole, thank you for sharing your stories and always being here for me. Then and now. To my beloved son Tyler. Thank you for being a part of my life. You are my greatest joy.

Contents

.

BOOK I

Eula and Elijah's Story

Elijah noticed the ebony beauty the moment he walked through the stained-glass doors. He had seen her at different youth programs. Captivated, he stood frozen in time—until he heard the agitated whispers of his mother's voice demanding him to take a seat. To avoid his mother's glare, he reached for the old, torn song book.

"Will all visitors please stand and state your name and home church," said the scrawny lady at the podium. Elijah sighed; he always hated this part of church service, standing and waiting for the onslaught of strangers to greet him. He thought about escaping to the bathroom but knew his parents would be greatly disappointed. Elijah thought, *I wish we could just visit and sit quietly in the back.*

When the introductions reached their pew, Elijah's father proudly introduced his family and The Great Missionary Baptist Church as their place of worship. Watching how proudly his father spoke of his family and their church home,

Elijah understood the importance of the church custom. After all introductions were made, the members of the church began milling around, welcoming their guests. Elijah knew the formalities would be over soon, so he greeted everyone as quickly as possible. He didn't want to miss his chance to meet *her*. His breath grew shallow, and his heart began beating faster; he was sure the entire congregation could hear it as she approached their pew. As he extended his hand, her father gently pushed her forward. Their eyes met shyly. For the moment that was enough; he knew their paths would cross again.

"Elijah, come on, we're going to be late," Ace said. Isaac earned the name Ace because he had it all. A chiseled body, good looks, and he could get any girl he wanted. The two boys met in middle school during football tryouts and had been inseparable ever since.

"Ace, do you think she will be there today?" Elijah asked.

Ace decided to mess around with his friend a bit. "Man, who are you talking about? Janet, Melissa, or Cynthia?"

"Stop playing, you know who I am talking about," said a very focused Elijah.

"Look man, it is not a question of if she will be there; after all, 'The Leaders of Tomorrow' conference is being held at her church. What you need to worry about is how will you get past her bodyguard?" Ace said.

"I have a plan." Ace started to interrupt. "Wait, hear me out, you see my plan is…" Elijah took a deep breath before he continued, "I need you to work your charm on her sister Shiloh, to get her away from Eula."

"Ok, I'll give you five minutes. You know I have a reputation of only going out with swans," Ace said.

Grinning from ear to ear, Elijah responded "That's all I'll need." They spotted the sisters as soon as they entered the room.

"Let's do this," Ace said as he walked boldly toward them. He introduced himself, making sure he kept his focus on Eula's guardian. He boldly took Shiloh's forearm and escorted her to the punch bowl. Eula saw her admirer walking towards her. She thought *Oh no, he is headed over here. What a beautiful smile. Don't be nervous!*

"Hello, my name is Elijah," he said. Smiling, Eula leaned forward and said, "I know; we almost met before." They both laughed.

"I am Eula. Sorry about my parents; they are very strict, especially my mother."

"I would be too if I had a daughter as beautiful as you," he replied. She blushed. "So, how old are you?"

"Oh, I am seventeen," he said as he glanced at his watch. He thought, *Time is running out and I may never get another chance. I am going for the gusto.* "When can I see you again?" he nervously asked in a voice that was suddenly high and squeaky-pitched.

"I am not allowed to date, but our churches are hosting a three-day revival together. Maybe we can see each other there?" she replied.

"I'll be there," he said. Elijah could see Ace and Shiloh returning. "I guess I better go before your sister returns." Eula nodded her head in agreement. "Well, it was nice talking to you."

"It was nice speaking to you as well."

"How did it go?" Ace asked.

"Better than I expected. Hey man, thanks again. Are you ready to blow this place?"

"Yeah, let's get out of here."

"Elijah, my dad is more understanding. It's better if you connect with him," she said as he walked away.

Elijah patiently waited by the entrance of the sanctuary for the arrival of the Washingtons. He thought *Just remember, a firm handshake and direct eye contact.* Elijah quickly wiped his sweaty hands against his black trousers as the Washingtons entered. He took a deep breath and gave Mr. Washington a firm handshake with steady eye contact. Albert Washington held a great deal of influence in the church community. He sat on the board of directors for the League of Baptist Leaders and was a charming man with well-above-average looks. Mr. Washington was tall with a reddish-brown skin tone and jet-black wavy hair.

"Hello Mr. Washington. Welcome to the revival," said Elijah. Feeling a bit taken aback by the young man, but also impressed, Mr. Washington replied "Thank you son." Unsure what to say to Mrs. Washington, Elijah tilted his head and said hello. She smiled and moved to catch up with her husband. Esther Washington was a petite woman with striking features. She had the most amazing green eyes and a yellowish-brown complexion. Many in the church considered her the most beautiful woman in the entire county. Unfortunately, she had a reputation of being somewhat prudish and unfriendly, so most of the church ladies steered clear of her outside of the church.

It was the final evening of the revival and the atmosphere was electrifying. The stars were shining especially brightly; they seemed to be putting on a cosmic show for the congregation. They were twinkling and glittering in a perfectly synchronized dance. The youth group was excited; their entire program was set to take place under the stars. There would be no tents, chairs, or conventional boundaries. This night was more about the rekindling of old friendships and the emerging of new love.

With only the light of the moon, Eula slipped into the darkness to meet Elijah. She anxiously made her way to the butterfly garden. When she arrived at the gate, she was relieved to find her beau waiting. Elijah took her in his arms. "I can hold you forever," he whispered. But when he felt her push away, he released his embrace and took her hand. They moved slowly towards a large sycamore tree.

Elijah removed his jacket and made a place for her to sit. "I don't want this night to ever end," Eula said.

"Me either," he replied. "Eula, why don't your parents allow you or your sister to date?" he asked.

"I think my dad would be ok with us dating; it's my mother who is against it," she continued. "Can we talk about something else? This may be the last chance I will ever get to see you alone." Elijah wanted to confess his true feelings, but he thought *maybe she is right, this could be their last time together.*

"I hope that's not so," he said. They spent the rest of their evening talking about their hopes and dreams. "Close your eyes. I'll be right back," he said. Elijah had noticed a flower bush close by and took off to pick a flower for his beloved. "Hold out your hands," he said.

"You don't have anything creepy, do you?" she asked.

"Don't you trust me?" he replied.

She held out her hands and he gently placed the flower into her palms. When she opened her eyes and saw the delicate flower, she leaned forward and kissed him on the cheek. "I never want this night to end," she said. Eula was shocked that she spoke her thoughts aloud. Feeling bashful, she lowered her head. Elijah lifted her chin and looked into her eyes and said, "Me either."

It was at this moment he knew he was in love. Feeling the tension rising, Eula said, "We should get going." She left first to rejoin the group. Elijah followed shortly afterward.

"EJ, you haven't been the same since the revival, what is going on with you man?" his best friend asked. They walked in silence a bit before Elijah spoke.

"Ace, man, I just can't get that doll off my mind." Ace thought, *Oh, here we go again.*

"Well, what are you going to do about it? I mean it's been about two weeks since the revival. EJ, either you put up or shut up," Ace said.

"I know, you're right; I just don't know what to do. It's not like I can just go up and knock on her door." Elijah continued, "You know, she told me to focus on talking to her dad, but how do I do that?" He turned toward his friend, looking for an answer.

"I may just have a solution on how you can get on the old cat's good side. I saw him at the barber shop last Saturday. He was sitting in Ole Man Mack's chair. Isn't Mack your barber?" Ace asked.

"Yes, he has been my barber since forever," Elijah replied. "But what if," EJ started to say, but Ace interjected, "Hey Daddy-o, you're bringing me down. Let's go and shoot some hoops and we will figure it out."

Ace picked up the basketball and the boys took off running. Ace was right; as the boys were playing a game of one-on-one, Elijah relaxed, and they were able to devise a plan. They decided to elicit help from Elijah's barber. Mack Dancing was his name, but everyone knew him as Ole Man Mack. He was trustworthy, insightful and had an uncanny instinct about folks. So much so that many sought him out for advice.

Elijah desperately wanted to be Mack's first customer that day, so he rose earlier than normal to do his chores. Elijah was so deep in his thoughts he nearly jumped out of his skin when his mother touched him on his shoulder. "Son, where are you off to so early this morning?" his mother asked.

"Oh, good morning Mom, I didn't hear you come in." Elijah gave his mother a hug. Ruth Johnson was a compassionate, courageous, and soft-spoken woman. She was undeniably the strength behind her family. Her attributes gave her an inner beauty, incomparable to her physical beauty.

"What's on your mind, son?"

Elijah was stumped for words. He didn't want to lie to his mother, but he was not comfortable speaking to her about Eula yet.

"Nothing, Mom, I just want to get to the barber shop early before it gets too busy," he said.

"Um hmm, what is her name?" she asked. Elijah turned towards the door; he couldn't face her. "Elijah, turn around and look at me," she demanded. He imagined her standing with one hand on her hip. And she was, but something was different. It was like she read his every thought. Not wanting to embarrass her son any further, she offered to fix him breakfast.

"No Mom, I really need to get going. But I'll grab an apple," he said.

"Good morning, Mr. Mack," Elijah said as walked into the barber shop.

"Morning young man," he replied, "Looks like you're my first customer. Hop in my chair. I'll be with you in a moment." When he returned, he was dressed in a crisp white barber's jacket. He adjusted his chair so Elijah was facing the mirror directly. "So, what will it be today?" he asked as he wrapped the thin paper tissue around Elijah's neck.

"Just a little off the top and taper my sides," he replied.

"That's a lot, young man. Who's the lucky girl?" Mr. Mack asked. Elijah tried to keep his cool but Ole Man Mack was staring dead at him. He couldn't hide; his reflection had exposed his secret. Breaking the long silence, Mr. Mack asked if he wanted a shave. They both laughed. Mack pumped the pedal on the chair a few times that lifted Elijah and proceeded to cut his hair.

"Her name is Eula Washing…" The opening of the door distracted his thoughts; he continued after he saw it was only the paper boy. "Washington, and she has the prettiest green eyes." He paused, thinking about the first time he looked into them—she was just a doll, a real doll!

"So, what's the problem?" Mack asked.

"The problem is her parents are very strict!" Feeling exasperated, he dropped his head into his hands.

Ole Man Mack put his clippers down and got eye-level with Elijah. "Youngblood, everything's going to be just fine," he said. "Now tell me everything that has happened," Mack instructed as he continued to cut his hair. Talking to Mack was so easy that before long he had shared his deepest feelings for Eula. This was something he knew he could never do, even with Ace. Mack didn't say much as Elijah poured out his heart. He just nodded from time to time. This suited Elijah just fine; he was just glad to release his burdens. Ole Man Mack removed the apron and said, "Come back around 3 o'clock." Elijah knew not to ask any questions; he paid his barber and split.

Elijah eagerly entered into the barber shop. When he found Ole Man Mack's chair vacant, he started to feel nauseous. He heard a voice calling him and he looked over towards the curtain. "Go ahead, he is expecting you," said another barber.

"Come on in, take a seat," Mack said

"If you don't mind, I'll stand," Elijah replied

"Suit yourself, here's the scoop: In two days, meet Mr. Washington here. He will be expecting you around noon."

Elijah was so excited he lunged forward, grabbed Ole Man Mack's hand and started shaking it vigorously!

"Thank you, thank you; how could I ever repay you?" he asked.

"Calm down Youngblood, just see that I get an invitation to the wedding," Mack winked.

"Yes, sir," he happily answered. Elijah took the long way home; he wanted time to think about the meeting with Mr. Washington. He felt pretty confident that he could win over Mr. Washington but wasn't as sure when it came to Mrs. Washington. *This may be my only opportunity*, he thought. *I need to make a good impression. I'll need to speak with Dad tonight after dinner.*

Michael Johnson noticed that during dinner his son was distant and despondent. Which was odd, because normally this was his son's favorite time of the day. They would spend hours jawing about world and local events. Sometimes their friendly debates would last for hours. Michael Johnson was a successful business owner. He turned his father's mom-and-pop store into a lucrative business. He had such a magnetic personality that he seemed larger than life. Out of all the things

Michael achieved, he was most proud of his family. He was a loving husband and father to his two children.

"Son, is there something on your mind?" he asked.

"Ugh, no Dad, not really," Elijah replied. Mr. Johnson looked puzzled by the response until he remembered the discussion earlier in the week with his wife Ruth.

"How about after dinner you and I go for a walk," he stated. Elijah nodded. The night was ideal; the moon was in its full expression and provided perfect lighting through aligned oaks. While he waited patiently for his son to speak, Mr. Johnson spotted a scaly piece of tree bark. He picked it up and began to gently separate the wood with his hands.

"This will make a nice piece for a carving, son," he said, hoping to break the silence.

"Dad, I am going over to meet with Mr. Washington." He paused. "To ask for permission to see his daughter. I want to make a good impression, but I am afraid he might say no," he blurted out.

"Son, just be yourself, you're a fine young man and I am sure Mr. Washington will see that," he replied. Sensing that something else was bothering his son, he continued, "Elijah, you're a good son with a good heart. When you meet Mr. Washington, be honest and state your intentions."

Elijah smiled and said, "What if he says no?"

"Then you go back and ask again and again until he says yes," he chuckled. "Do you know how many times I had to ask your granddaddy for permission to court your mother?" Before Elijah could answer, his dad replied "Plenty." Mr. Johnson put his arm around his son's shoulder. "Now tell me all about her."

Dad was right, Elijah thought. *If I want something, I must be willing to do whatever it takes, even if I have I to ask a hundred times.* Just the thought of asking more than once made Elijah anxious. He jumped out of bed and started pacing back and forth, running every possible scenario in his mind. *This isn't helping,* he thought. *I wish I could call her.*

Time was moving at a snail's pace; he woke up at the top of every hour. *This is brutal,* he thought. *I need to get some rest. What would Mom do? Ah, a glass of warm milk.* While it warmed, he thought more about what his dad had said earlier. *Just be myself and state my intentions and everything will work out.* Elijah chuckled; his dad always had the best advice. Feeling relieved, he turned off the stove burner and headed to bed without the milk. *Just be myself,* was his last thought.

When Elijah turned the corner, he found the man that he hoped would be his ally sitting on a wooden bench reading the newspaper. The two men respectfully shook hands and started walking down the boulevard. Albert Washington didn't waste any time; he got right to the point of their meeting. "We are going to give you our permission to court Eula." Elijah remained cool. He knew there was more.

"However, son, I want to fore-warn you, Mrs. Washington is reluctant on the idea. But I reckon you can change her mind." Albert didn't wait for an answer. "Can we expect you at dinner this Sunday?"

"Yes sir," he replied. Elijah walked away feeling both ecstatic and confused by Mrs. Washington's attitude. He couldn't figure out if it was personal or just the way she was. Elijah decided it was worth the hassle to see Eula.

Against her better judgment, Esther agreed to allow the Johnson boy to call on their youngest daughter. Her husband was very persuasive with his argument. He pointed out their eldest daughter Shiloh's tragic status as a spinster.

Shiloh was a tall and lanky girl as straight as an ironing board. She was a beautiful girl who had inherited her parents' striking features but unlike her mother and younger sister, she didn't seem to care about her appearance. She rarely wore make-up and her entire wardrobe consisted of black, grey and white hues.

The one opportunity Shiloh had for happiness had closed. Esther sent her beau away, saying he was not good enough for their daughter. After that Shiloh lost interest in dating and what was worse, her suitors were few and far between.

"The young man will be here shortly. Are you ready?" Albert asked his wife.

"I just don't trust that boy. I know he is up to something," Esther replied.

"We have already been through all of your doubts and agreed to have him over for dinner," Albert said. "Besides, the boy comes from a good family."

"I just don't trust him," she said and turned toward her mirror. She privately thought, *That boy was up to something; always too polite, Ma'am this and Ma'am that.*

"Esther," Albert called.

"Yes, dear," she mumbled.

"I am going downstairs, please hurry," he said as he walked out the door.

Eula couldn't sit still. She kept pacing the floor. Shiloh burst in the door with widespread arms. "Your Prince Charming has arrived," she said. The girls both started to laugh. They were close despite their age difference. Eula felt sorry for her sister, always having to escort her around town. She didn't understand why no boys ever came to visit Shiloh.

"Well, what is going on down there?" Without pausing to catch her breath, she continued, "What's Mother saying and how is she acting?"

"You know how Mom is, but Dad seems to like him," she said.

"I sure hope you're right," Eula replied.

Moments later they were called to come down for dinner. Eula rushed to the door like a steam locomotive. Shiloh jumped in front of the door to slow her baby sister down.

"I know you're excited, but if Mom thinks you're smitten with him, she will put an end to this immediately," she warned. Stunned by this revelation, Eula looked at her sister and questioned why. Shiloh only words were "Trust me. I know." They both walked out of the door and walked downstairs gracefully.

Three steps from the bottom, Eula got her first glimpse of Elijah. He was patiently waiting in the foyer with her parents. He was wearing a dark brown suit with a mustard-colored tie. She believed her heart was going to explode. But remembering what Shiloh had said earlier, she contained her emotions. When she reached the last step, he stepped forward and held out his hand to assist her down. He eagerly presented the flowers he had hidden behind his back to Eula. She looked towards her parents for permission before she accepted them.

The Washingtons were pleasantly surprised with the scope of Elijah's conversation. He was well-versed on many subjects. His table manners were exceptional, which pleased Mrs. Washington. After dinner, Eula invited Elijah to have lemonade on the porch. They both headed toward the swing seat that sat two, but decided against it and sat in individual rocking chairs.

"Do you think they are watching?" he asked. They both laughed at the question.

"I think you may have won my mother over," Eula said.

"I sure hope so; she is one tough cookie," he stated. "You look very pretty tonight," he said.

"So, do you. I mean, you look handsome," Eula shyly replied.

When Mrs. Washington passed by the window for the third time, he took that as a clue to wind down his visit. "It's getting late, and I don't want to overstay my welcome," he said.

"I am glad you came," she replied. Awkwardly they stood there, looking into each other's eyes, wishing they could embrace. When they thought no one was looking, they briefly touched hands.

As Elijah's visits became more frequent, their love for each other grew. It was getting more difficult for them to contain their feelings. The only freedom they had to express their affection was when Warden Shiloh was on duty. She always turned a blind eye, giving them more liberty than she ever had had.

Eula couldn't believe what she was hearing over the school intercom. She had won a position on the Homecoming Royal Court! Her classmates started cheering and chanting her name. Eula could barely contain herself in her seat. Thoughts of her and Elijah freely dancing the night away—without the watchful eyes of her parents—invaded her mind.

"Congratulations, Eula. Now children, take your seats, you'll have plenty of time after class to wish her well," Mrs. McDougal said.

Eula found it hard to concentrate for the remainder of the class. She began thinking about a personal victory. One that would give her and Elijah time alone. Being part of the Homecoming Court was the perfect opportunity.

"Mom, where are you?" Eula yelled as she burst through the front door. "I made the Homecoming Court," she continued. All the commotion startled her mom.

"What's going on child?" Esther asked. Eula tried to speak but could barely catch her breath. "Calm down and tell me what's going on," Esther said.

Eula took a deep breath. "I made the Homecoming Court!" she said.

"That is wonderful news baby," Esther said as she embraced her daughter. "Now quiet down and tell me everything; remember, you're a lady and should always act accordingly."

"Yes ma'am," her dutiful daughter answered. In a relaxed tone Eula told her mom all of the duties of the royal court. She went into details about the attire for the game. However, she was a bit hesitant to mention the dance. "Mom, part of the honor of being elected is the homecoming dance," Eula said. She noticed her mom's facial expression change at the mention of the dance.

"Oh, please Mom can I go?" she asked.

"I'll talk it over with your father," she replied. Esther was proud of her daughter's accomplishment, even though she believed Eula should've won the Homecoming Queen spot. *She is growing up too fast* is all she kept thinking.

The girls pounced on their dad as soon as he opened the door. He was barely in the door when in unison they blurted out something about a homecoming court and dance. He chuckled and looked over at his wife, whose expression was less than enthusiastic.

Turning back to his girls he asked, "What's all the excitement about?"

After telling her father all the good news, Eula asked "Oh, Daddy please can I go?"

"Your mother and I will discuss it," he said as he kissed them. Albert sat down next to his wife and took her slender hand into his.

Esther spoke first. "I think she is too young. I don't mind her going to the football game, but the homecoming dance is just too much."

"Esther, she is sixteen and not a baby anymore. Honey, you're going to have to let go. She is a good girl," he said. Albert leaned in to hug his wife, but she twisted slightly and rejected his comfort.

"What if she asks if that boy can take her?"

Before she could finish her thoughts, Albert interjected and said "He is back to being *that boy* again? He is a fine young man. Who would you have her go with? Shiloh?"

"Well, why not Shiloh?" she retaliated.

"Don't be ridiculous honey, Shiloh is not her babysitter," he replied, visibly agitated. Esther knew her husband had made his decision and her baby girl would be escorted to the dance by Elijah. Defeated, she left the room with her head hanging low.

Elijah arrived promptly to pick Eula up. Mr. Washington answered the door. "Good evening, she'll be down in a moment, I guess," he chuckled. "Young man, you better take a seat, they may be up there for a while," Mr. Washington said.

Aww, I got it, Elijah thought. The men both laughed. Both men stood up when they heard the commotion from above. When Eula entered into the room, Elijah was taken aback by her beauty. Elijah had to control his urges to hug her and nervously presented the corsage. His hands were shaking as he pinned it on. He knew if made a mistake Mrs. Washington would call the whole evening off.

Once outside of her parent's view, Eula asked "Why were you so nervous?"

"I knew if I pricked you in anyway your mother would persecute me!" They both laughed as they walked toward Elijah's car. And like a true gentleman, he opened the car door. Eula imagined her mother was watching his every move, looking for anything to condemn him.

The gym had been magically transformed. The old wooden bleachers had been retracted and covered by dark felt fabric and adorned with hundreds of handmade glitter-covered stars. High above the room more images of the constellations hung from the ceiling. Rows and rows of circular tables led the way to a magical dance floor. Iridescent lighting illuminated the atmosphere, creating a heavenly, starry, winter wonderland night.

Elijah began slowly walking toward the seating for the Royal Court, all the while thinking he didn't wish to be one moment without her. Eula gently tugged his arm, signaling him to stop.

"What's wrong?" he asked.

"I am not going to sit with the Royal Court. I am going to sit with you," she said.

"Are you sure?"

"Yes, I just have to be here for the group dance and photo." Beaming with joy, he softly squeezed Eula's hand as he searched for the most secluded table.

Elijah watched as his beloved performed the waltz. She moved so gracefully. *I am a lucky guy*, he thought. Once the dance was over Elijah jumped to his feet and met her on the floor. The band began playing up-tempo music and the auditorium became alive. The students were gyrating and jiggling all over the place. When the band slowed down the music, Elijah pulled Eula in close to his chest and held her captive as they rhythmically swayed side to side.

Eula leaned in closer and whispered, "Can we go someplace where we can be alone?" Shocked by her own boldness, she held her breath, waiting for his response. Elijah immediately reached for her hand and escorted her off the dance floor. They gathered their things and left the enchanted room.

"You trust me?" he asked. Eula nodded. "I want to take you to one of my favorite places. It's where I go when I want to think things over," he said. Eula smiled within; no one had ever made her feel so special. They drove until the lights of their small town faded. As Elijah turned onto the gravel road, the reflective metal posted sign read City View Lookout Point. Written in graffiti just below were the words *Lovers' Lane.*

Once the car was parked, they fell into each other arms. Elijah began kissing her gently, starting with her forehead and moving downward towards her lips. Goosebumps ignited her spine. She briefly thought to pull back, but her feelings were so overpowering. When their lips touched, she gave way and parted hers. The kiss was like sweet, soft cotton candy. She could have rested there forever. He pulled back. They sat quietly, until their eyes met and spoke the desires of their hearts. Their passion was too hard to ignore. Neither wanted to disappoint her parents, but the longing for each other was undeniable. Moments later they succumbed to their desire.

Eula never told anyone about the night she lost her virginity. She shared most of that magical evening with her sister but left out the intimacy part. One morning while getting dressed, she noticed that her breasts were fuller and tender to the touch. She began to panic. Eula burst into Shiloh's room and dove onto her bed.

"What's the big idea?" Shiloh asked. Eula didn't reply; she buried her head deeper into the pillow, crying silently. Shiloh gently turned her little sister over and started to wipe away her tears. She held her until her weeping subsided. Eula slowly raised up from her sister's protective arms and told her everything. Shiloh cuddled Eula's face in her hands and kissed her on the forehead.

"I know of lots of girls who do it all time and they never get pregnant! I only did it once!" Eula sobbed.

Eula left for school early to meet with Elijah. He was sitting in a swing when she arrived. She took a seat next to him. "Elijah," she paused, "I am expecting."

Looking confused, he asked, "Expecting?"

She sighed and took a deep breath. "I am pregnant."

Not knowing what to say, he reached out and embraced his beloved. "Eula, I love you and will never leave your side.

I can't believe it. When did you find out? Have you told your parents yet?" he asked.

"No, and I don't know what or how I am going to tell them. I have told Shiloh. She will be with me when I tell my parents," Eula said.

"I want to be there too, if you don't mind," he replied.

"I don't think that's a good idea. I will do this alone," she said as she stood up to leave.

"Eula, wait! I really think I should be by your side. I mean what will your parents think, especially your mother, if I'm not there with you?"

"I'll be ok, trust me; now I really must go."

"Okay, if you believe that is best, but if you change your mind I'll be there," he said. Elijah watched Eula as she walked away. Not knowing what to do, he decided to sit awhile longer to gather his thoughts. *What will my parents say? Will they be disappointed in me? What would they say when they learn I didn't stand by her side, when she told her parents?* His thoughts were out of control; he could barely catch his breath. He did the best he could to calm his mind. *Where do we go from here? I wished Eula would have stayed so we could talk things over a little more!* Feeling angry and frustrated, he picked up some rocks and started chucking them. *No matter what happens, I love Eula and I will be there for her. God give us strength*, he prayed.

Elijah broke the news to his parents that evening after dinner. They were disappointed. They had hoped he would be settled with a job before marriage and children. They wanted to call the Washingtons right away but after their son explained Eula's wishes, they agreed to wait.

With Shiloh by her side, Eula knocked on her parents' bedroom door.

"It's open, come in," her mother said.

Shiloh and Eula stepped in and stood silently. When the girls didn't speak, Mr. Washington asked, "What's going on girls?"

"Mom, Dad. I think I am pregnant," Eula said in a barely audible whisper.

"What?!" her mom yelled.

Shiloh held her sister's hand a little tighter. "I think I may be pregnant," she said again. Albert walked over and hugged his daughter.

"Why is Elijah not here by your side?" he asked.

Before she could answer her mother interjected, "Because he has abandoned her, used her to get what all boys want. I kept saying that boy was no good, I knew he was up to something," her mother grunted as she turned away from Eula.

When her mother finished, Eula softly said "I asked him not to be here. It was my decision, not his." No one spoke for a few minutes.

Albert sat next to his baby girl and said "I am not happy with the situation, but we will be here for you, no matter what the circumstances. Now go to your rooms so I can talk with your mother," he said.

Albert closed the door behind him and took a few deep breaths before speaking. "Esther, I know it's not what we had planned for our daughter but…"

"But what, Albert?" Esther said. He knew not to speak yet. "How can you act so casual about this? Our sixteen-year-old daughter is pregnant!" she screamed.

"What will you have me do, berate her as you are doing? What will that solve? Esther, our daughter needs us, can't you see that?" Albert said.

"Oh, I see you have already made up your mind and as usual you're taking their side. Tell me this. What type of life will she have?" she asked.

"The same kind you're having," he replied. *Damn, she just keeps pushing and pushing until I just can't take anymore of her nonsense! She has been so afraid Eula would make the same mistake she did. And she did. But the difference between us is, I don't see my daughter or my grandchild as a mistake! All I know is she will not do to Eula, what her mother did to her!*

"How dare you Albert, you are always throwing my past in my face. What about yours?" she asked.

"Baby, your past is my past and I am not ashamed of it," he said.

"What about Shiloh?" she asked. "Do you have any other children out there?" she asked.

"You know I don't. Had I known Dinah was pregnant, I would have done the right thing by her as I did by you. I was just as shocked as you were to learn that I had a daughter," he said.

"So you say," she said.

"Esther, be mindful of your tongue. I am not the only person with a secret, and I am tired of you throwing mine in my face. I appreciate you treating Shiloh like she was your own daughter, but you were not exactly pure when we married.

"Esther, I have never lied to you. It's you who likes to keep secrets! If it was up to me, I would have told Shiloh the truth about her mother. I love my girls equally the same," he said as he stormed out.

◆

Shiloh did the best she could to console her sister in the days that followed. "Eula, your baby will come out with a frown if you don't stop moping around," she said in a teasing manner.

"Shiloh, it's been a week and Mom will not even look at me. She hates me, what do I do?" she cried.

"It'll get better. I promise. Now let's get ready. Elijah and his family are coming to dinner," Shiloh said. "Seeing him will help you with this."

"I know, it feels like I haven't seen him in months," Eula smiled.

"Months? Try a week! You are so always dramatic," Shiloh said, smiling, as she closed the door.

Moments later, Eula heard a knock on the door. Thinking it was Shiloh, she jumped up and flung open the door with the biggest smile. Her mother stood outside her door. "Mom, I thought you were Shiloh," she tried to say.

"Never mind all that and what do you have to smile about? I am very disappointed in you. You have brought shame to our family. I blame your father too, always giving in to you girls," she said. Eula didn't have the courage to stand up for herself, but when her mother started to speak ill of her father, she found courage.

"Mom, don't blame Father for my mistakes," she replied.

"Don't you dare sass me, child!" she said. "That boy and his family will be here shortly. I don't want to see you sulking around here!" she instructed.

"Yes, ma'am," Eula replied.

When the Johnsons pulled into the driveway, Esther's attitude changed; the scowl on her face disappeared immediately. She called her husband to answer the door as she took a seat on the sofa. As the Johnsons entered, she stood to greet them. They all exchanged pleasantries but wasted no time getting to the heart of their gathering.

Eula and Elijah sat in the backyard as their parents discussed the matter at hand.

"Eula, don't you think we should be part of this conversation? I mean, they're deciding our life. I am going to go in there. Are you coming?"

"No, it doesn't matter what I want," she softly replied. *My mother will have her way, like she always does.* Hand in hand, the young couple walked into the room.

In a matter of moments Elijah's and Eula's fates were sealed. Albert and Esther insisted that Elijah step up and do the honorable thing for their daughter. The Johnsons agreed. It was decided that once they were married, they would live with the Johnsons. Everything was happening so fast. Their entire lives were being planned without any input from them.

Elijah tried to reason with them. "Mr. and Mrs. Washington, out of respect, don't we have a say in what we want?"

"It doesn't matter what you want. I am doing what is best for my daughter and maybe you should have thought about that before...you decided..." She paused; she couldn't get it out of her mouth.

Elijah's parents spoke up. "Esther, we understand how you feel, but our son is here, and he will do right by your daughter."

"Mom, you and Dad please know that I love Eula. I am just asking that we be included in the decisions," Elijah looked at his parents; he knew this was not their doing.

Eula excused herself and went outside to breathe. Elijah followed. Elijah wasn't opposed to getting married, but he wasn't sure of Eula's true feelings.

"Eula, we don't have to get married if you don't want to. I love you. I fell in love with you the first time I saw you. I will love our baby too. I promise to always take care of my family. It will be our decision," he said.

"I love you too, and yes I want to marry you, but I feel like we are being forced to marry." She paused. She didn't know how much of her true feelings she wanted to share. She could hear her mother voice saying, *What happens in this house stays in this house.* She decided not to betray her mother again. She tucked away how horribly her mother had been treating her.

"I like your mom. I am glad we will be staying with your parents."

"Eula, are you ok?" he asked.

"Why do you ask?"

"Don't get me wrong, but why would your mother not want you to stay in your home with her? I mean, this should be a special time for a mother and daughter, right? I know this decision was not my parents'. Why would your mother abandon you when you need her the most?"

"I don't know." *How can I tell him my mother is more concerned about how she is perceived by others, and I have shamed her!*

Elijah never wanted Eula to be hurt again. They walked in silence in their private thoughts. Elijah took a few blades of grass and made a makeshift ring. "Eula, stop; I want to ask you something."

When she turned around, she found Elijah on bended knee. "Eula, will you marry me?"

Without hesitation; "Yes, oh yes!" Elijah put the grass-made ring on her finger. "Eula, I'll replace this one very soon."

Two Sunday dinners later, Eula and Elijah were married. It was a small private church ceremony; only family members were invited.

After the ceremony everyone returned to the Washington's home.

"Shiloh, I am scared," her little sister confessed.

"I know you are, but you have to be strong for your baby. Mrs. Johnson seems like a nice lady," she said.

"Mom won't even look me. I know I made a mistake but why does she hate me so much?" Eula asked.

"Mom will come around," she said. "Babies always have a way of making things right."

"Then why is Mom kicking me out? It's like she doesn't want anything to do with me or my baby." Eula knew her sister couldn't answer her questions, but it felt good to air them out.

"I don't why she is kicking you out Eula, but I know she will come around."

"I sure hope so," she replied.

Just then, her father asked "Eula, where are you?"

"I am in Shiloh's room," she said.

"I'll be right up," he said. "Knock, knock," he said as he opened the door. Shiloh excused herself.

"Daddy, I am so sorry for all the trouble I have caused our family," Eula cried.

"Baby girl, you have nothing to apologize for, we love you," he said.

"Then, why is Mom not here with you, Dad?" she asked. Albert thought, *How can I explain to our daughter why her mother is not here supporting her?*

"She will come around, I promise," he said. "Now wipe those tears away. The Johnsons are waiting," he said.

"Ok, Daddy," she cried. Eula gave her daddy and sister one last hug before she got in the car. She kept hoping that her mom would come down from her bedroom and say goodbye. But her mother never appeared.

"Please tell Mrs. Washington goodbye and we will pray that she feels better soon," Mrs. Johnson said.

"Knock, knock, can I come in?" Ruth asked.

"Yes," Eula replied.

Ruth took a deep breath before opening the door. *Dear Lord, I hope this child has an appetite today. Thank God, nothing came of the blood found in her urine.* "Hello honey, are you feeling better today?"

"Yes," she replied.

Ruth gently sat on the bed next to her daughter-in-law. "Eula, your doctor wants you to gain a few more pounds before your next visit."

"I am trying," she said.

"You know, you gave us quite a scare when you started bleeding."

"Sorry, I didn't mean to. Mrs. Ruth, I am so glad you were able to take me to the emergency room. I mean if it wasn't for you and your husband, I don't know where I would be now."

"Child, I can't say I understand your mother or her ways but right now your only focus should be on your baby. Eula, you're young and healthy and the doctor couldn't find anything wrong with you."

Ruth tenderly stroked her tiny face. "Honey, the thought of anything happening to you or my grandbaby . . . well I don't know what we would do. And think about how your parents would feel to lose you or your baby."

"What about them? My mom doesn't care about me!" she sobbed.

Ruth cradled Eula in her arms and began rocking her, while whispering "Let it out baby."

"She never comes over to see how I am doing. I know she hates me and probably this baby too!"

"Now, your mother doesn't hate you or the baby. *[Although she privately wondered if she will ever come around?]* Would you like for me to talk with her…"

Before she could complete her thought, Eula interjected, "No ma'am!"

"All right then, we have to get your weight up before your next visit. So, do you want breakfast, lunch or dinner?" Ruth asked.

"I would like some blueberry pancakes," she replied.

"Blueberry pancakes coming up. You need help getting to the restroom?" she asked.

"I think I can make it, and Mrs. Johnson, thank you for all you have done," she replied.

Eula sat at the edge of the bed for a few moments thinking about how kind Mrs. Johnson had been to her. *I probably would have lost the baby if it wasn't for her. Lord knows I have been sick from the beginning. First the awful nausea and vomiting, then the bleeding and who knows what's coming next? I am blessed to have her by my side*, she thought.

Elijah was woken by the yelping sounds from his wife. "Elijah, wake up! Come quickly!" she demanded. "I think the baby is coming."

He quickly jumped out of the rocker to his feet. Overwhelmed and filled with fear at the sight of Eula's pain, he stood in a daze staring at her. "Elijah! Stop staring at me and do something!"

Elijah yelled for his mom, who had been sleeping close by, expecting her daughter-in-law to give birth at any moment. "Go wake your father and call the Washingtons and the midwife." And, just to keep him busy, she told him to boil some water.

She found her daughter-in-law slumped over the bathroom sink. "Come, let's get you cleaned up and comfortable." She took her by the hand and led her to the bed. She placed an extra-large nightgown on her and propped a few pillows behind her.

"Are you comfortable darling?" she asked. Eula just nodded her head. "Now darling, can you tell me how long ago your water broke?"

"I am not sure," she paused as another contraction passed through, "but I think about 30 minutes ago." Ruth called down to her husband to bring some ice.

The doorbell rang. Ruth prayed that it was Nadean the midwife; as best she could tell Eula's contractions were coming about 4 to 5 minutes apart. She knew it was too late to get the child to the hospital, so her first grandbaby was going to be delivered here in her home.

"Thank God, you're here," she said to Nadean as she entered the bedroom.

"How are you doing Eula?" the midwife asked. Eula was sweating profusely and in the midst of a contraction. "Ruth, how far apart are the contractions?" she asked.

"Well as far as I can tell, her labor pains are increasing to about every three minutes."

Nadean checked her cervix; it was dilated 9 centimeters.

"What's wrong?" Eula asked.

"Eula you're doing just fine," Nadean replied.

"Is my mother here?" the panting mother asked.

"Yes, she just walked in," Ruth said.

"Now Eula, I need you to listen and do as I say," the midwife commanded. "The baby will be here shortly. I will tell you when to push," Nadean said.

She grunted. "I need to push!" she screamed.

"Hold on Eula, not yet . . . Now, Eula! The head is crowning! I need one more push and you're done." Eula roared like a lion and pushed with all her might! Moments later she heard *It's a girl!* followed by the sounds of healthy lungs. They swaddled the baby in some warm cloths and handed her to her mother.

Elijah heard the cry of his child. He immediately ran up the stairs in a flurry of excitement to meet his child. Looking down at his wife with the baby in her arms, he fell to his knees next to them. "It's a girl," she mumbled. "Hello Eva Kaye Johnson."

BOOK II

Eva Kaye Johnson's Story

E va was a lovable baby, always cooing at anyone who gave her the slightest attention. When Eula returned to school, Ruth took care of Eva. Eula had hoped her mother would help her mother-in-law, but all her pleas fell on death ears. Ruth often reassured her that spending time with her granddaughter was a joy, not an imposition.

One day while washing the dishes, Ruth watched as Eula walked up the sidewalk. Judging by her slumped-over posture and how she dragged her feet as she walked, she knew Eula had visited her mother. Ruth thought, *I am so glad the baby is asleep. I will never understand how a mother could hold such animosity toward her child.* As Eula entered the house, Ruth asked "Hello. How was school?"

"It was ok."

Ruth thought, *I can't stand to see this child in so much pain. I'll take a chance and see if she will open up.* "How is your mother?"

"The same, she never asked me anything about the baby. I know she is mad at me, but I wish she wouldn't take it out on Eva. All she ever talks about is church and sinners."

Ruth was at a loss of words. She knew she couldn't say what she really felt. Besides, she didn't want to add to Eula's pain. "Come here, precious." Ruth wrapped her daughter-in-law in her arms as Eula wept.

"Elijah honey," Eula whispered early Easter morning.

"Is something wrong with the baby?" he asked.

They both lay still so as not to wake Eva. "No, the baby is all right, he or she is just doing a number on my bladder. We need to talk about moving into our own place. Eva will be two years old soon and with the new baby on the way, I am afraid there is not enough space for our growing family."

"I know you're right but," he paused.

"But what?" Eula asked.

"I was thinking my parents are so attached to Eva; I just know it's going to kill them if we move out."

One of the things she loved about her husband was his compassion for others. "Honey, I will miss Ruth too, she has been like a mother to me, but I am sure she will understand. So, we will break the news after church today?"

"Yes, after church."

"Ruth, honey you really outdid yourself today, dinner was outstanding," Michael said.

"Yes, it was," the rest of the family chimed in.

Ruth thought, *I am a blessed woman, to have such a loving family.* "I hope you saved some room for dessert. You have a choice of German chocolate cake or peach cobbler *a la mode*," she said.

"I'll have a little of both," her husband said.

And as usual the rest of the family echoed, "Same for us!"

"I'll help you, Ruth," Eula said. When the women were alone Ruth asked, "Are you feeling ok? You hardly touched your dinner."

"I am feeling ok," Eula said. She thought, *I wish I could just tell her now before Elijah chickens out.* "Ruth we will take care of the dishes; you have done far too much today." Eula solicited her husband's help with the dishes; she didn't want him alone with his parents and risk the possibility of him chickening out.

Elijah asked to speak his parents when they finished. "Mom, Dad, do you have a moment, we would like to talk to you," Elijah asked.

"Of course, come and sit down," his father replied.

Elijah hesitated, he didn't know exactly how to start the conversation. "Dad, you see with the new baby coming, we thought, um I think…"

Eula interrupted; she couldn't bear watching Elijah struggle. "Mom, Dad, what Elijah is trying to say is, with the new baby coming, we need a bigger place."

Michael and Ruth looked at one another and smiled. "Son is this what you were babbling about? We understand your family is growing and you need your own space. I am going to miss my grandbaby, but we understand," Ruth said.

Eula and Elijah sighed. As usual, Ruth gracefully put everyone at ease. "Besides, your dad and I have been discussing it as well. The Bryants are moving in a few weeks and your father and I spoke to them about buying their home." Without waiting for a reply, she continued. "Now it's a lot smaller, but we think it's perfect for your growing family."

Eula thought, *this is going better than she expected.* "I like it!" Eula said. Elijah looked at his wife. He hadn't seen her this enthusiastic in a long time.

"Eula, don't you want to see the place first?"

"Yes, but I already know it will be perfect. Eva will still be close to her grandparents and besides I love this neighborhood."

"Thanks Mom and Dad, we will take a look at it tomorrow," Elijah said.

Elijah and Eula, just like everyone else on the block, admired the outside of the Bryant's home. Their yard was always well-manicured. They decorated for every season. At Christmas the neighbors would marvel at the festive lights and decorations.

When they entered inside it was love at first sight for Eula. The home was warm and inviting, every piece of furniture was a perfect fit. The décor was subtle yet bold, exciting yet reserved. Eula squeezed Elijah's hand as Mrs. Bryant continued with the tour. When the tour was over, the young couple waited in the kitchen while the deal was worked out.

"Elijah, this home is perfect for us, but I know we can't afford it."

"Eva, listen don't worry, let's just wait and see what my parents negotiate.

"Honestly, we don't know if they are selling or renting."

"You're right, your parents are so generous. I just wish they didn't have to do everything for us."

"Eula, I didn't want to say anything until we found a place, but your father has agreed to help out."

Their first night in their new home was surreal. Much to their surprise the Bryant's left most of their furniture for the young couple. Mr. Johnson and Mr. Washington agreed to pay the mortgage until Elijah could take over.

Shortly after they moved in, Eula gave birth to their second daughter, Beth Ann Johnson. They raised their girls in their home for the next four years. When Eula gave birth to their third child, Elijah Kenneth Johnson III, Ruth offered to take Eva in until they moved to a bigger house. Eula was reluctant at first; she didn't want to be separated from her children.

"Eula, have you thought about letting Eva come and stay with us? I know Elijah is working hard and cannot help out a lot, and three children is a lot to handle, and the toll the pregnancy took on you? Well, we were afraid we were going to lose you. Remember, the doctor said you need plenty of rest."

"Yes. I know you're trying to help, but the thought of my baby not being here with me is hard to imagine."

"I know it is and I completely understand. Baby, we are not trying to take Eva away, we are just trying to help you out. I am sure my grandson is keeping you up at night, boys are always a handful." Eula smiled.

"I know you're not, Mom, I just don't ever want my child to feel abandoned." Eula thought, *like my mother has done to me.* Ruth hugged her daughter-in-law. She knew her mother's behavior had affected her but hadn't realized just how much until now.

"Listen, you're not abandoning your baby. I'll keep coming here in the morning to help you get Eva ready for school."

"No, Mom, you're right, Eva should stay with you during the week. Thank you."

Eva's formative years were divided between her loving grandparents and her immediate family. On occasion her mother would take her to visit her Grandmother Esther and Granddaddy Albert, but she never felt welcomed by her Grandmother Esther; in fact, she would spend most of her visit with her granddaddy. One day Eva asked, "Mom why do I have to go and see Grandmother Esther, she is not like Grandaddy Albert."

"What do you mean Eva?"

"I mean she never says much to me, she just spits into her tin can."

I can't let her treat my child like this, I'll talk to her! Who Am I kidding, I can't stand up to her but I can stop the visit? Oh Lord give me strength. "Eva, how will you feel if we stop coming to Grandmother Esther's house?"

"What about Grandaddy Albert? I love him. Will I be able to see him?"

"I am sure that can be arranged."

Soon the visits to their house ceased. Her grandfather continued to visit Eva and his grandchildren every chance he got.

Eva was excited; she was turning sixteen-years-old tomorrow. She was the eldest of Eula's three children. She stood 5ft 4in with a curvy petite figure and golden-bronze skin that matched perfectly with her sandy hair. She had a bubbly personality with eyes that twinkled when she smiled. Her parents were giving her a party to celebrate.

"Eva, I am ready. Come down please. And make sure your hair is completely dry," her mom said.

"Ok," she replied.

The pressing of her daughter's hair was usually a joyous occasion for them. They laughed together and Eva would tell her mother about her school days and friends. But lately all her daughter wanted to talk about was boys. Eula hoped that by allowing her to invite some of the boys from church, her daughter would see that she wasn't as prudish as her grandmother. The evening started as usual as they chitchatted about one thing or another.

"Mom, can I ask you a question?" Eva said.

Oh Lord, Eula thought. "Yes, of course," Eula replied.

"Mom, when can I start to date?" Eva asked.

Eula took a deep breath and thought, *Dear Lord help me with an answer. She is too young to understand.*

Eva interrupted her mother's thoughts by saying, 'Please Mama answer me why not?"

Eula sighed. "Because I said so and that is all you need to know!"

"Yes ma'am," she sadly replied. Eva didn't say another word; she just sat sulking in the chair. As Eula brushed her daughter's hair she thought, *it's for her own good; one day she will understand.* As soon as her hair was done, Eva jumped out of the chair to find her father. She ran outdoors first, hoping to find him in the garage working on the car or something. She was disappointed when he was not there, because that was the one place she could speak with him freely without fear of her mother interrupting them. When she opened the garage door, she smelled the earthy scent of her father's cigar and knew right away the whereabouts of her dad. Eva flung the door open and jumped onto her daddy's lap as he sat in his den.

She began babbling hysterically about one thing to another, making it difficult for Elijah to understand her. He allowed his daughter to vent as he rocked her until she grew tired and fell asleep. She was so exhausted from crying that she didn't awaken and he carried her to her bedroom. While tucking Eva in, he prayed that God granted him the strength to talk with his wife about the treatment of their children, especially Eva.

Elijah turned off the light and closed Eva's bedroom door. He took a moment in the dark stillness to gather his thoughts. Resting his head against the door frame he thought, *I have given in to Eula's every demand in our marriage, but I cannot continue to allow her to be so harsh to the children. I want to keep my wife happy and allow our children to have fun and not be so restricted as we were as children.* Elijah drew in a deep breath and prayed for a peaceful discussion with his wife.

He could hear Eula frantically moving about in the bedroom. He paused and took a deep breath before opening the door. Elijah was shocked to find Eula in a state of chaos, her clothing, wigs, and jewelry thrown everywhere. It was like a tornado had passed through. He had to tiptoe through the mess and clutter in order to reach his wife. He took Eula's hand and led her to the foot of their bed. When she attempted to speak, he placed his index finger in front of his lips, motioning her to remain quiet. Elijah went to the bathroom to draw his wife a hot bath. He added her favorite bath salts and oils. When it was ready, he appeared in the doorway and silently extended his arm. While Eula bathed, Elijah began to place everything back into its proper place. Elijah sat up when Eula entered the room. "Are you feeling better, after your bath?" he asked.

Eula paused for a few moments. "She always runs to you. No matter what I do or say, it's never enough," she replied.

"Honey, come to bed and rest. I am sure Eva appreciates everything you're doing. Everything will work out," he said.

Elijah held his wife throughout the night and thought, *what has happened in her life that makes it so difficult for Eula to be vulnerable and to express love to the children? What shall I do? Considering her emotional state I certainly can't speak with her now about the children. Oh dear God, help me!*

The sunlight woke Eula up just moments before her alarm was to sound off. She quickly reached over and pushed the off button. She wanted a moment to just to lay with her thoughts. *How did I get here, how did I become so high-handed? My family hates me*, she thought. Tears began flowing out of the corners of her eyes. *Dear Lord, help me.*

Elijah started to move around. "Lay back down," he mumbled.

She wiped her tears away. "Good morning. No time to rest, it's our daughter's sixteenth birthday and I still have a lot of things to do." She rolled over and gave him a kiss.

"Ok," he muttered.

Eula decided to prepare Eva's favorite breakfast before she ran her errands. She set a plate setting with a sealed note with the words *Happy Birthday Eva* written in all capital letters. She tied pink balloons on the back of the chair. Eula thought, *I hope she forgives me*, as she closed the door behind her.

Eva woke to the sweet smell of blueberry pancakes. She leapt out of bed and made a mad dash to the kitchen. "Mom?" she called, but there was no reply. By the time she reached the bottom step her mouth was drooling with anticipation. "Mom?" she called again. When she turned the corner and saw the mountain of balloons, she smiled as big as the sun. Eva saw the note; she picked it up to read it, but quickly put it away when she heard her sister and father coming.

"Happy Birthday Pumpkin," her dad said.

"Yeah, happy birthday little sister."

"Dad, where is Mom?"

"Don't know, she was up with the chickens."

"I love birthdays," Eva said.

"Why is that, Baby Girl?"

"Because it's the one day that everything is all about me!"

After breakfast, Eva rushed to her room to read the letter from her mom. She took a deep breath before she started to carefully remove the seal. *Happy Birthday to My Beautiful Daughter,*

I hope all of your dreams come true, I know mine did sixteen years ago. It is my hope and dream that everything you desire in life comes to pass. I love you, signed Mom. Eva clenched the letter next to her heart and whispered I love you too.

The guests started arriving around 6 o'clock. Eva wanted to be there to greet everyone as they arrived, but Eula reminded her that a lady always makes an entrance.

"Elijah, it's time to get the guest of honor," Eula said.

"I am surprised she hasn't sent out a distress call," he said. They both laughed.

"Pumpkin, are you ready?" he asked. Eva opened her bedroom door. Elijah took a step back. "You look beautiful, Pumpkin." He fought hard to hold back his tears. "You look just like your mother did on our first date."

"Thank you, Daddy," Eva replied. Elijah wrapped his arms around her.

Eula gathered everyone around the stairs and as Eva made her entrance, they all clapped. On Eula's cue they started singing the Happy Birthday song. When the cheering subsided a bit, Eva thanked all her guests for coming to her party.

"Mom, thank you, I am so happy."

"You're welcome, now go and have fun with your friends."

"Ok. Mom, thank you for the letter."

Eula smiled at her daughter. "Go on and enjoy your party."

"Good evening everyone, I apologize for interrupting your meeting," Pastor James said. "Sister Johnson, when you get a moment, can I have a word with you in my chambers?"

"Yes, Pastor, we were just finishing up," she said.

"Great, see you in a few minutes."

"Please have a seat Sister Johnson. Can I offer you something to drink?"

She thought, *Take a seat? What's going on?* "Huh, okay. Pastor, is anything wrong?"

"Nothing is wrong, Sister Johnson. I wanted to tell you, all that you do around the church has not gone unnoticed." Eula sat a little taller.

"Well, you know of course that I've been looking for a new deacon?"

"Yes, Pastor, any luck?" She didn't wait for answer. "Should I start making arrangements and contacting other ministers?"

"Well that depends on your answer," he said.

She thought, *my answer? What would my answer have to do with the preparations for selecting a new deacon?*

"Sister Johnson, I am offering the position to you," Pastor James said.

Eula stood up. "*To me*, Pastor? But the position is usually given to men."

"I know this is unprecedented in the Baptist church, but you have met all the criteria and have all the qualities I am looking for. You have impeccable knowledge of the Bible and your dedication to the church is above reproach. Plus, I know I can trust you in my stead. Should I continue?" he asked. Eula slowly sat back down.

"No Pastor," she replied.

"Pastor, I am so grateful for this opportunity! But I will need to speak with Elijah first," she replied.

"Of course, I certainly understand. You have until the end of the week to tell me your decision," Pastor James said, as he quietly slipped out the door. Eula knew what her answer was immediately, but out of respect for Elijah she would run the proposal by him. Driving home Eula thought, *Elijah would not stand in my way. After all, he had relinquished his role of patriarch of the family to me years ago and besides, he was a peaceful man whose main concern was the happiness of his family.*

Breaking the news was easier than she thought. Elijah was so ecstatic with excitement that he jumped up and gave his wife a whopping kiss. In the midst of the celebration Eula pulled back from her husband and gave him a perplexed look.

"What is wrong my love?"

"You didn't seem to have any concerns about the amount of *time* I will be away. Are you glad I will be away so much?"

Elijah wanted to say a lot, but knew his thoughts would fall on deaf ears. *How could he tell his wife, that if her mother hasn't forgiven her now, she probably never would? How could he tell her that she is becoming like her mother? How could he tell her that their children needed her love and acceptance?* But he knew the truth would fall on deaf ears!

Elijah looked into his wife's eyes and said, "No my love, we will miss you dearly. You have worked so hard for the church, and you deserve this opportunity." Elijah took his wife in his arms and assured her of his love.

"Hello guys, I am home!" Elijah said as he opened the front door. He could hear the jovial sounds of his children coming from the kitchen. He followed their harmonious vibration. He stopped just short of the doorframe and watched his daughters tease their younger brother. *It's been two weeks since Eula departed. I truly didn't know if the children would adjust, but it looks like they're doing just fine,* he thought. "Ahem," he cleared his throat before entered the kitchen.

"Hi Dad, we didn't hear you come in," they said in unison.

"Junior, what are you cooking?"

"It's my secret recipe."

"Oh, can I have a taste?"

"Dad, Dad, I wouldn't take a chance," Eva said.

"Yeah, Dad," Bethany echoed. They all burst out laughing.

"Son, please tell me that your secret concoction is not the only thing you prepared for dinner."

"Ah, Dad, us men have got to stick together, but to answer your question, no it isn't."

Elijah patted his son on the back. "Junior, I will always have your back. I am going to unwind a bit before dinner."

"I'll come and get you Daddy, when dinner is ready," Eva said.

Elijah sighed heavily as he rested his head against the soft Italian leather recliner. Over time his chair had given way to the contours of his body; it fit every nook and cranny of his physique perfectly. It was his perfect refuge.

As soon as he closed his eyes images of Eula flooded his mind. He sat back and enjoyed the memories of yesteryear when they first met and when their love was exciting. He thought, *the reality of those days are gone and she has changed. I wonder how Eula would react if she knew all the changes I have made with the children's routines.*

"Um, you have outdone yourself son, dinner was absolutely wonderful," Elijah said.

With an inflated chest Junior thanked his dad. Eva and Bethany started to pick up the dirty dishes. "Wait just moment girls, sit down. I want to speak with you all."

"Sure Dad," they replied.

"Dad, is everything ok?" Bethany asked.

"Of course, everything is just fine. I just wanted to check in with you guys to see how you're doing. How do feel about your mother's absence?"

Puzzled by the shift in their dad's behavior, they sat up taller. "I know this is different from what you're used to, but I do want to know how you're feeling. I think your generation calls it rapping, you dig?" They all laughed at his attempt to be hip. Bethany and Junior looked to their big sister to answer for all of them.

"Dad, we know you miss Mom and so do we, but honestly, we are fine. Dad, this time with you alone has been great. I mean, you actually want to hear what we have to say. Dad, can I ask you a question?"

"Sure," he replied.

"Do you think Mom would have ever taken the time to actually listen to us? Let us hang out with our friends? Have sleepovers? Dad, it's like you trust us!" Eva burst out.

Elijah was at a loss for words. He searched his children's eyes before he started to speak. He thought *I need to make them feel safe and secure.* "Ahem, so first of all I want you kids to know that your mother loves you dearly and she wants the best for you kids. Eva, Bethany and Junior come here." Elijah wrapped his children in his loving arms. "Things will get better when your mother returns, I promise, but for now let's enjoy our time together."

Friday after school some of Eva's classmates were going to the movies; something that she was never allowed to do. Eva paced back and forth, trying to think of the best way to ask her dad for permission. She didn't want him to think she was taking advantage of him; after all he had given them so many liberties.

"Dad, I'm home. Where are you?" she asked.

"I'm in the study," he replied.

"Um, some of the kids are going to the movies tonight and to the soda shop afterwards. Do you think I can go with them?"

Elijah saw the hope in his daughter's eyes and didn't want to disappoint her. He cleared his throat before speaking. "Pumpkin, who exactly are you going to the movies with?"

"I am going with Alice and some of her friends."

"Eva, is there any chance some of her friends might be boys?"

"Honestly, I don't know. She never said anything about boys."

"Eva, I want you in by nine o'clock."

Elijah watched as his daughter walked with the other girls and thought *Eva has so many of her mother's traits, and just like her she has a restless spirit that longs to explore the world.*

"Table for four please," Alice said to the carhop. Eva looked around. The atmosphere was electrifying; she could barely contain herself. Some of the kids were dancing to the tunes coming from the jukebox, while others were checking out the hottest cars.

Eva nudged her best friend. "Who is that cat over there?" she asked.

"Which one?" Alice replied.

"The one who keeps looking over here," Eva said.

"Oh, that's Fox, "she said.

"I have never seen him around school," Eva said. The girls all laughed. "What is so funny? "Eva asked.

"It's nothing really, but Fox graduated last year." Alice said. "Don't waste your time, church-girl, he is out of your league," her friend said.

"I am sure you're right," Eva said. Noticing the time, Eva looked at her friends and said, "I have to go."

Alice smirked and said, "You always have to go right when the fun is about to begin." Eva shrugged her shoulders and headed out the door.

A wave of guilt would settle in her spirit each time Eula returned home. She loved being an evangelist. It was a dream come true. Even though at times she was ridiculed by some for deserting her family, she loved doing the Lord's work. It was easy for her to ignore their comments as long as Elijah was supportive. Besides, when she returned home, everything seemed to be in place and the children seemed to be well-adjusted. She also knew that Elijah had loosened the reins and had given the children more freedom than she would have allowed.

"Elijah, I am home!" Eula said as she entered into their home. She had left the conference early so she could spend some time alone with Elijah. Elijah came barreling into the living room.

"You're early!" he said as he lovingly stroked her face. The two embraced in a passionate kiss. Elijah wanted to scoop his wife up, take her to their room and make passionate love.

Sensing his urges, she said "The children will return shortly!"

"I know, but they're going to bed early tonight!" he said. They both chuckled and settled with just holding each other.

"Elijah, I need to ask you a question and I want you to be honest with me."

"Ok," he replied.

"How are you and the children doing? Do you want me to quit the position?" Before he could reply, Eula went on to say, "I believe you have everything under control and the children look so happy. Are *you* happy, Elijah?"

Elijah turned toward his wife so that they were face-to-face. "My love, the children and I are doing fine and yes, I am happy. But more importantly I am happy to take care of our children. And I am happy that you are doing work you love."

Clearing her throat, she said, "The children do seem well-adjusted and my relationship with our children has improved, but I need to know that I am doing the right thing for our family."

Elijah leaned in and softly kissed his wife and said, "Yes my dear, you are doing the right thing."

Just then, the children came in. "Mom, you're home," they said in unison. Eula hugged and kissed her children.

"Now what have you'll been up to?" she asked. Eva wanted to share with her mother everything that she had experienced lately but knew all of it would come to a halt if she did. Instead, she told her mother what she wanted to hear.

"All right, you go and do your homework. Dinner will be ready at five," she said.

"Yes, ma'am."

"I have great news. I'll be home for the next few weeks," Eula happily announced.

"That's great Honey. Isn't it, kids?" Elijah said.

"Yes, that's great news Mom," Eva said. *My life is over*, she thought. "Can I be excused? I have a project I am working on."

They all quietly rushed into Eva's room.

"Do you think Dad said anything to Mom about our new routine?" Bethany asked.

"I don't think so," Junior said. "Eva, what do you think, will Dad talk to Mom about our new schedule?"

"Honestly, I don't think so. While she at home we are all doomed to bend to her will. Which means no more fun, sleepovers, movies or anything else. We can kiss them all goodbye!"

Eva screamed into her pillow when they left.

"Eva, have you asked your parents if you can go to the movies?" Alice asked.

"I have already told you my mother is back at home, and she will never allow it," Eva said.

"Well what about your dad?"

"My dad will only tell me to ask my mom, which will leave me in the same predicament," Eva replied.

"But Eva…" Alice started but was cut off midsentence.

"The answer is no, no, and no, so stop asking me Alice."

"Don't take your frustration out on me."

"I'm sorry Alice, I didn't mean to," Eva said. "It's just that as long as my mother's home, I'll be on house arrest," she said. They both laughed.

"Now tell me again, what did you tell Fox about me," she asked. Eva had to live vicariously through her friend Alice.

"That's old news. Let me tell you the latest and greatest," Alice said.

"Go on," she said. Eva loved her best friend dearly, but sometimes she could be a drama-queen.

"Well guess who has her sights on Fox," she said.

"Who?" Eva asked.

"Tanya Dubois!"

"What!" Eva screamed.

"That's all I know right now; I'll keep you posted. I gotta go, my mom wants to use the telephone. Bye."

The news angered Eva. She thought *I am going right now to their room and demand that Mom stop treating me like a baby. It's just not fair that all we get to do is go to church!* She stopped just short of her parents' bedroom. *What's all the commotion coming from her parents' room?* She walked slowly to the door to listen.

"Eula, you know I support you completely, but I am concerned about Eva. I think she may have questions that only a mother should answer. Besides, you just got home and told our children you would be home for a while," he said.

"The kids will be fine," she said.

"Damn it! I am not opposed to your precious work, as long as it doesn't interfere with our family!" Elijah screamed.

"Honey, I am sorry, I didn't mean to upset you. I know this is a last-minute project, but I promise, I'll make it up to you and the kids," she said.

"Who is over this project?" he asked.

"My mother recommended me," she said.

"That explains everything," he said. The room fell silent. Eva ran to her room. She had never heard her parents argue.

With her mother away on her "precious project," all Eva could think about was how she could finagle her father into allowing her to stay out later. She didn't quite know what her father's concerns were, remembering the conversation she overheard, but she did know how to play up to her daddy. All weeklong Eva was on her best behavior; she even cooked dinner twice that week. By the time Friday rolled around Eva could ask for the world and her daddy would oblige.

"Hello Daddy. How was your day?" she asked.

"It was fine, just fine," he replied.

"Daddy, dinner is ready."

Elijah gave his daughter a dubious look. He knew she was up to something.

"Daddy can we change my curfew time on Fridays?" She continued without a pause. "All the other kids get to stay out until midnight. Daddy, you wouldn't have to worry about me getting home because I can ride home with Alice."

"Eva, we will give it a try; I am not making any promises."

"Ok, thank you Daddy."

Eva took special care when she dressed today. She wore her yellow dress with the sweetheart neckline, knowing it was sure to catch Fox's eyes. And it was working. When Eva arrived at Doug's Burgers and Soda shop, a number of boys hurried past her to open the door. Alice spotted her friend as soon as she entered. She began calling and motioning Eva towards her booth.

"Wow," Eva exclaimed. "I can't believe how crowded Doug's is tonight."

"Eva, girl, it is always busy on Friday's; you're just usually gone by this time." Alice said. Eva just smiled at her friend's candid remark.

"Are you sure he is coming?" Eva asked.

"Yes, I am sure. He said he wanted to talk with you tonight," Alice replied.

"How do I look? I am just so nervous," Eva said.

"Calm down and relax!" Alice said as she leaned in closer to her friend. She continued, "He is headed your way, play it cool."

They all exchanged pleasantries. Alice sat with her friend until the agreed-upon clue was given. "The weather is starting to warm up," Eva said. Alice politely excused herself. Eva and Fox sat in the booth for hours sharing their personal stories. Eva discovered that he was two years senior to her, which made him more intriguing and alluring. Sitting with Fox made her feel like a princess. After all, she was with the handsomest boy in town. She thought, *Eat your heart out, Tanya Dubois.*

From a distance Eva saw her best friend pointing at her watch. She nodded.

"Is everything ok?" Fox asked.

"Yes, why do you ask?" Eva anxiously answered.

"Because you just looked engrossed in thought." Eva shyly smiled.

Right on cue, Alice interrupted. "Eva, we have to go."

Fox stood up and softly held her hand and said, "Until next time."

Once they were out of sight of the soda shop, Eva grabbed her friend's hand and thanked her for making it a magical night. Eva made it home before her new curfew.

"Eva the phone is for you," Bethany shouted.

Eva picked up the phone in the hallway. "Hello," she said.

"Hey girl, what have you been up to?" Alice asked.

"Hold on a second. Bethany, hang up the phone." Once Eva heard the click of the other receiver, she continued. "Oh, nothing much."

"Ahem, excuse me, who do you think you're fooling. It's me, your best friend," Alice said.

Eva paused. She didn't know how much she wanted to share with her. "Alice, I swear to God if you say anything, I'll kill you."

"I would never say anything, cross my heart and hope to die."

Eva took a long deep breath. "I've been secretly seeing Fox."

"What? For how long?"

"We have been seeing each other for about two months. I don't know if you remember, but you helped set it up," she said.

"You mean the night you guys met at Doug's? Wow, that has been awhile. I can't believe you didn't even tell me, the one who made all of this possible!" They both started laughing. "Where do you guys meet?"

"Usually at the park. But sometimes he picks me up around the corner from the house and we just drive."

"Alice, he's very nice but…"

"But what?" Alice asked.

"Sometimes I feel pressured."

"Pressured?"

"You know what I mean," she replied.

"Listen Eva, you don't have to do anything you don't want to do. You heard what happened to Maryellen?"

"No, what?"

"She is pregnant, and her parents are sending her away."

"We haven't even kissed," Eva said.

"I gotta go, my mom is calling me," Alice said.

"Ok, bye," Eva said. Eva couldn't help but think about Maryellen. She thought, *poor Maryellen pregnant. I wonder who the father is.*

The first time Fox leaned in to kiss Eva, she was so jumpy and excitable that they bumped noses. They each chuckled for a brief moment before Fox moved in again; however, this time he gently guided her head in the right direction. Eva's nervousness dissipated as soon as their lips met. Suddenly, she was swept away in array of emotions and feelings she never expected.

"Eva, can you stay out a bit longer?"

Lowering her eyes, she softly said "Fox, you know I want to, but my father would never allow it."

Fox pulled away and said, "You know I really like you, right?" Eva nodded her head as Fox continued, "Why can't you stay out late like the other girls? I mean, I always see Tanya out late."

"Fox, I have already explained why I can't stay out late! So, go be with her, if that's what you want!" Eva screamed. Before he could say anything, she took off running.

"Eva, come back," he pleaded.

When she was clear from the sound of his voice, she stopped to gather her composure. She reached in her pocket for her handkerchief and began to wipe away her tears. Eva kept thinking about what he said, *"I always see Tanya out late." Does this mean he is seeing her too?* Distraught with the thought of losing Fox, she began to sob out of control.

Monday at school Eva confided in her best friend about what Fox had said concerning Tanya. "Alice, you're out late; do you see them together?" Eva asked.

"No, he usually hangs out with the guys. But everyone knows she wants him and will do whatever it takes to get him!" she replied.

"Whatever it takes, Alice?" Eva asked.

The bell rang and the girls departed for their next class. Eva couldn't concentrate on her studies; her thoughts were inundated with Fox. She enjoyed spending time with him. She liked it when they kissed and when he caressed her breasts, but to go any further was terrifying.

After school Eva ran straight to her room and slammed the door. *My life is over*, she thought as she plummeted to the floor. Sitting with her back against the wall, she cradled her legs in her arms and rested her head on her knees. She began blaming everyone from her mother to Tanya Dubois for her problems with Fox. She thought, *if only Mom wasn't so strict, I could see Fox every week and wouldn't have to worry about Tanya*!

"Eva come here," said Elijah for the third time. He thought, *what is going on with her, she seems to always be preoccupied.*

"Daddy, you called?"

"Yes, and what took you so long to respond child?" he inquired.

"Sorry Daddy, I was reading," she awkwardly smiled.

Elijah took a long, disappointed look at his daughter before saying, "Dinner is ready." Just as he suspected, someone had caught his daughter's attention and the lie she just told was the evidence. He wanted to call Eula and demand that she come home right away. But he knew his pleas would fall on deaf ears.

"Knock, knock, Eva can I come in?" Elijah asked.

"Sure, Dad," she said.

"Baby girl, I want you to know that you can talk to me about anything. And I know something is bothering you," he said.

Eva thought, *I can't speak to my dad, he would surely pull in the reins.* "Dad, everything is ok. I am just cramping a bit," she said.

"Ok, if you say so," he sadly replied.

Eva agreed to meet Fox at his house, even though Alice advised her not to. On her way over she rehearsed in her mind how the conversation would go. *I'll give him an ultimatum, its either me or her!* When he opened the door all her anger disappeared. He pulled her in and started kissing her with unbridled passion. Her mind was in a battle with her body. "Fox," she whispered, "I can't do this."

"Don't you love me?" he said.

"I do but..." she started to reply.

Fox, sensing and anticipating her fears, pulled out his weapon of deceit, and assured her that she would not get pregnant. Even though she wasn't clear as to how someone became pregnant, she believed him and gave into his desire and her curiosity.

Afterwards they laid silently in each other arms.

"Eva, are you ok?" Fox asked.

Why would he asked me if I am ok. Did I do something wrong, she thought?

"Yes, of course I am fine. Why, is there something wrong?" she asked.

"No, it is getting late, and we need to get you home."

Fox parked his car inconspicuously around the corner from Eva's house and walked her the rest of the way home. Fox stopped short of Eva's house and leaned in for a kiss.

"When can I see you again?" he asked.

"I don't know, maybe next Friday," she said.

They became the hottest couple at Doug's Shakes, Malt and Burgers. Eva became a regular at Doug's with Fox by her side. They would meet up just to show their faces then discreetly disappear.

Immediately after rising from the toilet bowl, she was confronted with her reflection. She attempted to look at herself, but the shame and guilt was unbearable. She quickly sat down on the edge of the bathtub to think. *We have been going out for three months and each time my period came! Why didn't I listen to my friend instead of Fox; she told me the pull-out method was no guarantee! How stupid of me to trust Fox and how will I tell my parents? They will hate me for this!* In a desperate plea, she cried out to God, "Please make this not so!"

Eva chose to tell her father first, hoping that he would somehow soften the forthcoming impact. "Hi Daddy, can I talk to you?" she timidly asked.

"Yes, Pumpkin," he replied. Eva always loved it when he called her Pumpkin. She instinctively sat on her daddy's lap and buried her head into his protective shoulders. He knew his daughter was fearful of something.

"Daddy," she whispered, "I am pregnant."

Elijah's heart broke at that moment. Eva sunk her head deeper into her father's shoulders.

He stroked his daughter's head and said, "Everything will be all right, Pumpkin."

Eva gave a loud sigh of relief. "Dad, I can't face Mom alone; she is gonna be so angry! Can you be there please?"

"Sure," he replied. "Your mother will be home soon. Go up to your bedroom, I'll call you when we are ready." Elijah poured a glass of scotch before he sat in his recliner. He thought, *this is the one nightmare we didn't want any of our children to ever experience. Maybe if we would've told her the truth about our marriage she wouldn't be in this predicament. Eula is always trying to hide the past, just like her mother did.* Elijah sat further back in his chair and waited.

The humming of Eula's car's engine woke Elijah out of his stupor. "Kids, Elijah, I am home. Where is everyone?" Eula asked.

"I am in the study," Elijah answered. The pitter-patter of her heels sent his heart racing. He jumped to his feet, spilling his drink in the process.

"Elijah, what's going on, are you drinking?" She thought, *I can't remember the last time I've seen Elijah drink. This can't be good.*

"Eula, there is no easy way to say this, but I need you to…"

"You need me to what?" she interrupted.

"I need you to put your work aside and come over and sit next to me." He tapped the spot next to him. He took a few deep breaths and said, "Eva is pregnant."

"What!" She exclaimed.

"Our daughter is pregnant," he repeated.

Eula leaned back into the chair. She turned to her husband and said "This is all your fault; you gave her too much freedom. Can you imagine what the church members will say? I'll be ruined!"

"Eula, I don't give a damn about what others think, our daughter is pregnant and needs us!" He screamed. Neither one of them spoke for a while. "Eula, I tried to talk to you about Eva, don't you remember?"

"Oh, you're saying it's my fault. You said you could handle the kids and the household. I had my work," she replied.

"When did you become so priggish? Don't you remember how you felt when you were her age?" he asked.

Eula refused to answer his question. She got up to leave.

"One last thing before you leave. Eva needs us and you will make some time in your busy schedule and speak with our daughter," he demanded.

It was the first time Elijah ever spoke to her in that manner. Eula abruptly left the room. Eula avoided her daughter for a week, refusing to acknowledge her presence or assist her during her morning sickness. She thought, *Let Elijah take care of his precious princess.*

Eula cleared the house. She asked Elijah to take the children to Bible studies so she could speak with Eva. "Come here Eva," her mother called.

"Coming," she nervously replied. She prayed that her mother would find it in her heart to forgive her. *After all, isn't that the Christian thing to do?*

Eula was forceful in her attack on her daughter. She immediately began screaming obscenities and Bible verses at the sight of her. With each harsh word spoken Eva's vitality and zest diminished.

She cried out, "Mama, Mama I am sorry! Please forgive me!" But her pleas fell on deaf ears. Eula continued with her tongue-thrashing until every belligerent thought had been unleashed. Towering above her daughter, Eula instructed her to stand up and stop crying.

"It's too late to cry now," she said.

Eva was exhausted but did as her mother instructed. Time seemed to stand still as her mother pondered how to set atonement for Eva's sins. Out of the darkness of her thoughts, Eula skillfully began unfolding her wicked plan. She would do to Eva what her mother had done to her. Eva's marriage would squash gossip and Eula would not lose her standing in the church. It was hard for Eva to fully understand everything her mother was saying but the one thing she clearly understood was that she would marry Fox.

Eva did not want to marry Fox, but felt she had no other choice. So she agreed to her mother's proposal without regard to her feelings. She didn't have the strength to go against her mother's will; besides, not even her father, her *champion*, would go against Eula's agenda. Eva's only hope was that Fox would refuse to marry her, but she soon found out that Fox and his family were no match for Eula either. At the tender age of seventeen Eva was married and gave birth to a baby girl. Lela Kaye Grey had arrived in this world.

BOOK III

Lela Kaye Gray's Story

With the help of his parents, Fox was able to secure a small one-bedroom apartment. It wasn't much to look at, but at least they had a place of their own. Fox thought, *I hope Eva can look past the exterior.*

"Fox is everything ready at our new home?" Eva asked.

"Pretty much." Fox wanted to tell her it was nothing like what she was accustomed to, but he didn't have the heart to burst her bubble.

The exit nurse knocked as she entered, "All ready to go," she said. "Mrs. Grey, do you have any questions before we discharge you and the baby?"

"No ma'am."

The nurse wheeled them to the car and once she saw mother and baby securely in, she departed. They drove in silence for a while, each in their private thoughts. Fox thought, *I need to tell her about the house before we arrive. It's now or never.*

"Eva about the house, well it's nothing like what you're accustomed to."

"I am sure it'll be fine as long as we are together." When they pulled into the driveway Eva had to cover her mouth to keep from gasping in shock. From the outside it looked like an old, boarded-up shack. *This is what my life has come to*, she thought.

"Eva this is temporary, we will move into something better soon."

The first year of their marriage went by quickly. As Fox promised. they moved into a bigger and nicer apartment. Lela was growing so fast; Eva couldn't believe she was turning one in a few months. Even Eula started coming around—once they moved out of that shack. Eva loved being a wife and mother, but deep inside she felt like she was missing something. She had lost touch with her friends. The dreams she had for her future were lost. She sighed. When she heard Lela moving around, she knew her free time was over.

"You think Mom is going to come to Lela's birthday party?" Bethany asked.

"Who knows, she was pretty pissed at Fox for not having Lela's party at her house."

"What do you mean *was* pissed? She still is!" They both started laughing. "What is the deal with the two of them anyway?"

"You know Mom hasn't forgiven him for getting me pregnant and I don't think she ever will."

"Okay, I get that, but what is Fox's deal? Sometimes he is just downright rude to her."

"I know. I think he blames her for taking his life away."

"I am so sorry Eva; I wish things were different for you."

"Me too. Now enough talking, we've got to get the decorations up."

"Lela's party was a success; don't you think Fox?" Eva asked.

"Yeah, it was ok."

"Just ok?"

"She's just one-year-old; she is not going to remember any of this."

"Fox, the first birthday party is more for the adults than the kids." Eva thought, *let me change the subject and tell him my surprise.* "I was thinking since we never had a real honeymoon…"

Before she could finish her thoughts, he cut her off. "We don't have the money for a honeymoon; not then, not now!" Fox stormed out the door.

Eva thought, *I should've known better to bother him about a honeymoon. I'll do better.*

When Lela turned a year-and-a-half , Eva decided to get a part-time job at the grocery store as a cashier to help out Fox. The job didn't pay much, but was just enough to take care of the small incidentals. But to Eva it was an opportunity to get out of the house for a few hours, especially since Fox had started staying away for longer periods of time.

Eva was laying on the couch playing with Lela, when she heard a car pulling up the driveway. She jumped with excitement, thinking it was Fox coming home. She peeked through the curtains but was shocked to find her father walking towards the house. She thought, *what is Daddy doing here this time of the night?* "Hello Daddy. What are you doing here so late?"

"Can't your dad come by and see his grandbaby?"

"Of course, Daddy." She kissed him on the cheek.

Elijah picked up his granddaughter and whooshed her in the air until she grew tired.

"I think she is ready to go to sleep," Eva said.

"I'll put my grandbaby to bed."

"Dad, would you like a cup of coffee?"

"Yes, just don't tell your mother I am drinking coffee this late."

He paused. "Eva, you know I am not one to beat around the bush, so I am just going to come straight out with our concerns. What is going on with you and Fox?"

Initially Eva thought to play dumb but knew that would just prolong the inevitable. "Dad I really don't know. He hardly spends any time with us and every time I try to talk to him, we end up arguing."

"Pumpkin, why didn't you come to me and your mother?"

"No Dad, that would only push him farther away and you know how meddlesome Mom can be."

"Eva, are you happy? Do you want to get a divorce?"

"No Dad, he is my husband and I do love him. Beside he does pay all of the bills."

"Eva that's what a man is supposed to do, to provide for his family. Darling, marriage is a partnership; he is not only responsible for providing, but he is equally responsible for the mental wellness of the family. Remember, you deserve happiness too. Now, I got to get going before your mother gets home." He winked.

"Bye Dad." Eva thought, *is dad right, do I deserve happiness too?*

As the seconds passed, it became harder to ignore the tension in the room. It was as thick and suffocating as dense fog. Neither wanted to be the first to speak the inevitable. Fox took the lead because he knew Eva didn't have the courage.

"Eva, I am not happy, and I know you're not either." He paused, giving her an opportunity to respond. When she didn't say anything, he continued, "I don't make enough money to provide for our family and I am tired of crawling to our families for help. I have enlisted in the Army, so that I can provide for our daughter," he said.

"You know my mother will never approve of us divorcing," she blurted out.

"Eva, you're nineteen now; you don't need your mother's permission! Baby, the Army will give me the opportunity to travel and see the world while learning a valuable skill. It's my best chance," he explained.

"What about Lela?" she asked.

"I'll always be here for our daughter; in fact, she is my inspiration to become a better man," he gently replied.

"What about me and the promise you made before God to me!"

"Eva, do you truly love me? If you didn't get pregnant, do you think we would be married now?"

"No, we probably wouldn't be married."

"We made a mistake and I fully accept my responsibility, but your mother forcing us to marry was wrong. I will always take care of Lela, but I will not live under your mother's thumb. I am not like your father."

She thought, *you're right, you could never be half the man my father is.* Eva sighed, defeated. She knew his decision was the right one.

"Eva, I don't have much time left before I leave. Can we draw a line in the sand and call a truce? I would like to spend these last two weeks home here with you and Lela."

Eva's first thought was to be sarcastic and say something hurtful, but she realized it would only make him leave sooner. "Sure, we can. I want what is best for Lela too."

In the beginning after Fox left, Eva enjoyed the quiet solitude of the house. The daily fighting and bickering had ceased. Eva enjoyed taking care of her baby, but felt she was missing out on her youth. Most of her friends had gone off to college or were attending some type of trade school. Her life had become predictable, unimaginative, and boring. Caring for the baby and working at a thankless job were the highlights of her day. *This can't be it. I want more!* she screamed inwardly.

"Eva, girl is that really you? I haven't heard from you in a month of Sundays, what's going on?" Alice asked.

"Hey Alice, how are you?" she asked as hugged her friend.

"I am good. I heard Fox joined the Army and left you and the baby," she said.

Laughing, Eva said, "You're still the same, straight to the point. Yes, he did leave but it's not like you think or may have heard," Eva explained.

"What are you doing tonight? How about going dancing?"

"I would love to go but I don't have a babysitter," she replied.

Alice had forgotten all about the baby and she awkwardly replied "Ok, call me later if you find a sitter."

Eva knew her mother wouldn't keep her grandchild; she was too busy with the church. Besides, every time she asked her to keep Lela, she was subjected to some condescending remark from her mom about how disappointed she was with Eva. She thought of asking her dad, but didn't want to infringe on his kindness, as he was always bailing her out. *I hate to ask Bethany at the last minute, but I really need a break*, she thought.

"I am glad you called tonight. It will do you good to get out of the house," Alice said.

"Eva, I am so glad you decided to join me tonight."

"I know, I was going crazy! I just couldn't take it anymore;

the solitude was draining the life out of me! Girl, it almost didn't happen. I had to beg Bethany to watch Lela. By the way, where are we going tonight?"

"I thought we would go downtown to Maurice's," Alice said.

"Hey, can we stop and grab a bite, I am starving!"

"We can grab a bite at Maurice's."

Eva couldn't remember the last time she had had so much fun. She was on the dance floor all night, even on some of the slower songs. It was nice to feel the warmth of a man again.

"Can I have this dance?" the tall, handsome man asked as Eva was leaving the dance floor.

Eva smiled. "Can I get a rain check?"

Eva joined Alice at their table. "Eva, you look so happy," Alice said.

"I am having a great time. We have to do this again and again," she said.

After an evening of dancing and drinking, Eva decided that if Fox was off enjoying his life, she would too. Every weekend they would gallivant from one party to another in pursuit of a good time. Rumors quickly began to circulate about Eva. They said she was a wild and irresponsible mother, leaving Lela with sitters for days at a time. Eva didn't care; she thought, *I am just having a little fun.*

"Attention!" The squad leader yelled. The men immediately fell into formation and the leader quickly took roll call. He saluted the sergeant and turned them over to his command. The sergeant was known to be talkative and today was no exception. It was his first three-day pass since joining the army. Fox was starting to feel anxious. He thought *how much longer is Sarge going to keep us here? I don't want to miss my bus home.*

Leaning his head against the window, Fox settled in for the long ride home. He thought, *this may be the only rest I'll get this weekend.* His heart was heavily burdened with how to convince Eva to allow his grandmother to raise Lela until she was stable. Exhausted, he eventually dozed off.

He could smell the sweet aromas of his grandmother's cooking as soon as he stepped onto the porch. "Mama," he yelled out. Mama Grey appeared from the kitchen with arms wide open.

"Fox, oh my baby," she cried out. Fox picked up his grandmother and twirled her around. "Put me down, you here," she said.

"Mama what smells so good? Is it ready? I am so hungry I could eat a horse," he said.

Mama Grey laughed; she thought *this boy hasn't changed a bit!* "Now go on and wash up for dinner. I'll call when it's ready; now get out of my pots," she replied.

He said, "Yes ma'am," as he left the kitchen.

Mama Grey was well-respected and a pillar of strength to many in her community. She was a surrogate mother to many wayward and abandoned children. She was known for her generosity and kindness— but also one who would tend to your "hind' if necessary.

"Mama, you outdid yourself, the Army doesn't have nothing on your cooking," he said as rubbed his stomach.

"I made your favorite for dessert," she said.

"No! You made your famous pecan pie?" Fox instantly grabbed the old hand-cranked ice cream maker from the cupboard and proceeded to the back porch. Mama Grey cleaned the kitchen while Fox churned the ice cream. "Mama, it's ready," he yelled.

Mama Grey sliced him a huge piece of pecan pie. Fox piled on a heaping scoop of ice cream.

"I see the Army hasn't curtailed your appetite," she said. "Fox, what is going on, you look like you're fretting about something."

Fox began to feverishly rock back and forth. He knew he couldn't stall any longer. "Mama, I am concerned about Lela," he said.

Mama Grey just nodded. "Eva is out partying all the time," he paused, "and it's not just that Mama. I feel Lela is too much for Eva to handle. Mama, I am not saying Eva is a bad mother, it just that we were so young when we got married; she was only seventeen. I just feel she wants more from life."

"What about her family, Son?"

"What about them," he interjected before she could finish.

"Don't they help her with the baby?"

"Mama, I don't want my baby around those people. I mean her father is ok, but her mother is…"

"Watch your mouth!" Mama interrupted.

"Yes, ma'am," he said. "Mama, I don't know how to ask you this, but can you help us with Lela? Can she come and live with you?" he asked.

"Son, I knew you two were too young and irresponsible to marry. For the life of me, I can't understand the ways of her mother. Have you talked this over with Eva?"

"No, not yet. I'm leaving tonight and will speak with her tomorrow," he said.

"If she is in agreement, I will take Lela in," she replied as she reached to hug her grandson.

Fox arrived at Eva's apartment in his dress uniform. He thought that if she saw him well-dressed, she would fully understand why he left. Although he still had the key to the house, he didn't feel he had the right to barge in. When she opened the door, he was still taken aback by her beauty.

"Hello Eva, how are you?" he timidly asked.

Her blood instantly began to boil. *How dare he come over, dressed like that?* "I am fine," she snapped.

Fox attempted to move in for a hug, but Eva quickly moved to the side and allowed him in.

"Where is Lela?" he inquired.

"She is in her room," she said, pointing in the direction of their daughter's room. Fox visited with his daughter, bestowing her with gifts and love. He couldn't believe how much she had grown. Fox rocked his baby girl until she was asleep, then laid her down for a nap.

"Eva, there is no easy way to say this, but I am taking Lela to live with Mama Grey," Fox said.

"Who do you think you are? You can't just waltz in here and take my baby!" She screamed.

"She is my baby too and I want the best for her."

"And I don't?"

"Look, you're out every weekend drinking and having a good ole time. You leave Lela with anyone who is available, not worrying if they are suitable as babysitters," he said in a firm voice.

"What, am I supposed to stop living? You are the one who left us! I have a right to have a life too!"

"I didn't just leave; you knew I was going to enlist in the Army. I even postponed joining until Lela was three years old, per your request."

"Eva, we both agreed…"

She cut him off in midsentence. "No, *you* decided for both of us! You didn't care about our marriage! All you ever cared about was yourself and your precious military career."

"I am sorry. I never meant to hurt you," he humbly said.

Eva thought she would find relief after expressing her anger but all that surrounded her heart was more pain. "I don't care for your pity, not now, not ever," she spat at him.

"Eva, can you try to think about what is best for our daughter? Eva, I remember you had dreams too. Don't think of it as permanent. Mama Grey taking care of Lela will give you a chance to make something of your life too," he finished.

Eva stormed out the room screaming, "I don't give a damn about you or your military career! She is my daughter, and she is staying with me! You're not taking her anywhere!"

Realizing he couldn't reason with Eva, he slowly walked into the room and kissed Lela as she napped. "I'll be back later," he said as he closed the door.

Taking a seat in the diner where he first met Eva, he contemplated his dilemma. He thought, *I just can't leave Lela here with Eva, not in this situation. I wish I could've reasoned with her, made her understand that the best place for our child is with Mama Grey.*

The waitress interrupted his thoughts when she delivered his order. "Sir, is there anything else I can get you?" she asked.

"No, thank you," he replied. He immediately returned to his thoughts. *She has left me with no other choice. I am going to take Lela to Mama Grey.* At the thought of taking Lela away from her mother, his heart began to beat fast and even faster as he thought about the consequences of taking Lela from Eva. *What if she calls the police or worse, what if I am discharged from the army?* He thought about the consequences to his career versus Lela's safety. He decided, *it's worth the risk.*

It was the hardest decision he ever had to make. He knew he couldn't leave his daughter with Eva despite the potential risk to his army career. He just hoped one day Lela would understand why he took her away from her mother. Later that evening, while Eva was working, Fox entered into Lela's bedroom, bundled her up and headed to Mama Grey's house. He left a note next to Eva's nightstand with the words *God Please Forgive Me* on the front of the envelope.

10 years later....

Lela came flying through the back door. "Granny, I'm home! Where are you?"

"I'm in the parlor," she replied. "Come in here when you finish your cookies."

How did Granny I know I was getting a cookie? Lela laughed and thought, *Granny always knows what I am up to.* She shrugged her shoulders and went to her Granny's sitting room. "Granny, what's the matter, why are you looking so sad?" she asked.

Lela ran to her granny's side and dropped to her knees. "Granny what is wrong?" she asked again. Her heart started racing.

"Lela, I am ok. Get up and sit next to me," she instructed.

"Yes, ma'am," she replied.

Mama Grey reached for her granddaughter's hands and placed them gently between her overworked, aged hands. As she started to stroke them Lela looked into her granny's eyes; they were full of tears waiting to break free. It was then she knew the impending news was not going to be in her favor.

"What is the matter Granny?" She asked hysterically.

Mama Grey was never one to beat around the bush. She was always candid and forthright when dealing with folks, but when it came to Lela, she was at a loss for words. Finally, Mama Grey let out a long sigh.

"Lela, your mama wants you to come home and live with her and your sisters," she said. Lela looked perplexed. She wasn't sure if she was being given a choice.

"Granny, do I have to go?" she asked.

"Yes," Mama Grey replied.

"Why, Granny? Don't you love me no more?" Lela cried out. "I'll do better with my chores and my schoolwork Granny. I'll be a good girl!"

"Shh child," Mama Grey said. Mama Grey reached out and gently rested Lela's head against her bosom. "Of course,

I love you child, and don't speak that nonsense again, you hear me?"

"Granny, why doesn't anybody want me? Why was I given away?" she asked as she cried in her granny's arms. Mama Grey didn't know what to say. She didn't know how to answer her granddaughter.

"What about Daddy, does he know?" She desperately asked.

"The decision was made by both of your parents," Mama Grey said. *I knew this day would come, and my grandbaby would be taken away. Lord it's not my place to tell Lela what happened between her parents. Dear Lord give me the strength to release this baby back to her mother. I pray they can come together for the sake of their child. Amen.*

"Hello Mama Grey, this is Eva. How are you doing?"

"I am doing."

Eva thought, *she is just as ornery as ever.* "How is Lela doing? Did you get a chance to tell her?"

Mama Grey didn't have the heart to tell Eva that her child didn't want to live with her. "I reckon she will adapt," she replied.

"I am sure you're right. Mama Grey, her bus will leave in two weeks on a Saturday; you will be able to pick up her tickets at the will call booth. Well, I think that's about it, unless you have any questions."

"Nope," she replied.

"Ok. Bye."

Mama Grey held the phone to her bosom. She thought, *my poor baby*.

"Lela, dinner is ready," Mama Grey said as she knocked on her bedroom door. When Lela didn't respond, she opened her door. Lela lay perfectly still, until her grandmother was satisfied that she was asleep and walked away. Lela quietly reached underneath her pillow and pulled out her diary. She stared at the blank page, hoping to find words to express her pain. But her thoughts were hollow; all she felt was emptiness and uncertainty. She closed her journal and drifted off to sleep.

"Hurry up child, we are going to miss your bus," Mama Grey said.

"Yes ma'am," Lela answered as sat her suitcase down just outside her bedroom door. She turned to survey her room one last time. She looked over at the metal headboard frame where all her rag dolls rested their heads. She noted all the arts and crafts throughout the room. Each one of them held a special memory. Just before she closed the door, she remembered the nights when the old shutters would bang up against her window. She reflected on how Mama Grey would come to her rescue and assure her that everything was ok. She wondered if she would ever feel as secure in Oklahoma City as she felt with Mama Grey in Wewoka. As she gingerly entered into the living room the wooden floorboards were especially squeaky. It was if they were saying goodbye.

Lela looked over her shoulder one last time at the place she had called home. It was a small house made mostly of plywood. It was painted white with a bright yellow trim but today it too seemed to take on a gloomy glow. Lela quietly said goodbye to the only home she ever had ever known, then proceeded out the gate.

They walked in silence all the way to the bus station. Lela knew her grandmother was getting nervous when she started humming a church spiritual. Lela joined in. Lela had never seen so much commotion; people were moving in a fast-furious pace, nearly running each other over.

Mama Grey tugged her granddaughter's arm. "I need you to pay attention," she demanded.

"Yes, ma'am," she replied.

"Now don't forget in case of an emergency you have a nickel to make a phone call. Oh, and don't forget there is extra toilet paper in your knapsack." In the distance Lela could hear a loud humming sound. As she turned toward the direction of the sound, a big silver and blue bus with an image of a dog was pulling into the station.

Lela wished that she could be like the dog on the bus and just run away. The bus driver stepped off the bus and stood by the entrance of the door. He began bellowing out the bus destinations and boarding instructions.

Lela was thrust out of her thoughts and forced back into the reality of her impending fate. As Mama Grey moved in closer to the bus, Lela clutched her grandmother's sweaty hand with all her might. With tears flowing down her cheeks, she pleaded one last time for Mama Grey to allow her to stay.

"It's your mother who wants you home. And I have no rights to keep you away from her," she said as she gently wiped her granddaughter's tears away and ushered her onto the bus. When Eva turned around to say one last goodbye, Mama Grey had disappeared. Hurried by the other passengers, she quickly took a window seat and started searching the area for one last look at Mama Grey.

Lela was intrigued with the beauty of the different landscapes between Wewoka and Oklahoma City. In some towns, there were noticeable peaks and valleys, while other towns were as flat as a pancake. The one similarity was the scarlet dirt.

Moments before they reached the Oklahoma City county line, they ran into a strong, turbulent wind. The blood-red dirt violently swirled around the bus, forcing the driver to slow down to a snail's pace. Blinded by the residue, the driver was forced to pull over until the storm subsided. Lela shook with fear over this storm. She had never experienced anything like it, and she wasn't sure if they were in danger. A fellow female passenger—who had been secretly keeping her eye on Lela since they left Wewoka, got up and sat next to Lela.

"It's ok baby, it's just a little dust storm," she advised. Lela nodded gratefully and rested her head on the lady's shoulders. She fell asleep for the remainder of the bus ride. Too soon, the woman gently shook Lela. "We're here. Is this your stop?" she asked.

"Yes ma'am. Thank you for your kindness," Lela said. Eva was waiting when she stepped off the bus. Lela stopped in her tracks. She didn't know what to do or to say. Eva moved forward and hugged her daughter.

"How was your trip?" she asked.

"Just fine." Not knowing what to call her, she said Eva.

Eva smiled awkwardly. Eva hoped that one day she would call her Mom. They rode home in silence. They were both praying to God. One was praying for reconciliation and the other was praying for a safe return home.

When the car pulled up, her sisters Abigail and Deborah bombarded their older sister Lela.

"Stand back girls! Let her get out," Eva instructed.

"Hi, my name is Abigail."

"And I am Deborah," the other sister said.

"Hi," Lela shyly replied.

Lela knew she had other half-siblings and had met them twice. Once was when Eva brought them for a visit at Mama Grey's. The second time was at Grandpa Johnson's funeral in Wewoka. Lela unconsciously took a step back, *why did she keep them and not me. I can't see me in them, but I see my sisters in each other and Eva.* Lela looked back at her mother, then to her siblings. All she could think was, *why them and not me?*

"I'll explain later," Eva said as she touched Lela's shoulder in passing.

Lela was taken aback by how close the houses were. She had grown up with land all around and neighbors you had to walk or drive to see. She foolishly looked around for livestock but found not one animal, not even a chicken was to be seen. *City life was definitely going to be different*, she thought.

"Abigail, Deborah, help your sister with her belongings," Eva instructed. "Lela, I know this arrangement is different from

Mama Grey's where you had your own room, but I want you girls to really get to know each other like three peas in a pod."

"Yes ma'am," she replied.

"Girls, make some space for your sister's things," Eva said.

"But…" Abigail started to say something, until Eva turned around. Lela didn't see her mother's facial expression, but she could feel their resistance to having to share their space. Lela was equally disappointed with her new living arrangements. She realized that she would no longer have her own room or any privacy. She was glad she had left her rag dolls on the mantel in her old room.

Eva was so happy to have her daughter back with her. There was so much she wanted to say to her. "Lela, come with me. Abby and Deborah, I want you girls to have it all figured out when we return," Eva instructed.

"Yes, Mom," they replied.

Lela just followed. Eva gave her eldest daughter a private tour of the house. Lela noticed a small room off the side of the kitchen. It was filled with things that didn't seem to have a place in the home.

"Eva, what is this room used for?" she asked. Eva was saddened when Lela called her by her name. She thought, *I hope one day she will call me Mom.*

"I know what you're thinking Lela, but the decision has already been made; you will room with your sisters."

Eva replied, "Why can't I use that small room? I don't have much, besides they don't want me in their room. I hardly know them; it's going to be awkward."

"Lela, it's not up to them or you. I want you girls to get to know each other."

Lela angrily thought, *If that was the case, why didn't you ever bring them around to meet me!* "Do we have the same daddy?" Lela blurted out.

"No, their daddy died in a car accident a few years back and that's all I am going to say on the subject!"

"Yes ma'am."

Eva wanted to give Lela her space but thought it was better for her to bond with her sisters. *I surely hope she understands.* "Now go and shower; we are going to your grandmother's house."

"Is it far?" Lela asked.

"No, your Grandma Eula lives across the street."

Grandma Eula lived on top of the hill in a two-story white brick house. The house was strategically placed in the center of the neighborhood. The landscape was spectacular. There were lavender, lilacs, lilies, and pansies, ranging in every shade of royal purple with splashes of white Sweet Williams mingled in and filling the garden beds. From afar it looked like something out of a fairytale. The house was befitting of Grandma Eula's status in the community and church.

With such kindness, Eva took her eldest's hand as they crossed the street. As they got closer to the house, Lela noticed that the house seemed to have a gray shadow cast upon it. At the very top of the house in a small archway, she spotted a look-out window. It gave her the chills. Eula was sitting on her throne next to the fireplace. Eva went over and kissed her mother. Lela didn't move. She stood perfectly still until she was summoned.

"Send the child over," Eula barked.

"Lela, come and say hello to your grandmother," Eva said.

Lela started to move, but when Eula picked up her old coffee can and started spitting chewing tobacco, she stopped dead in her tracks. She had never seen a woman chewing and spitting tobacco. "Hurry child, I don't have all day," she said.

"Hello Grandmother Eula," she stuttered. The few times Lela had been around Grandma Eula, she had always felt uncomfortable, and this time was no exception.

"How is Mama Grey doing?"

Before she could answer, Eula abruptly instructed her to wait outside for her mother. Confused at her grandmother's sudden change, Lela answered, "Yes ma'am," and walked out the door and waited on the steps for her mother. Moments later, Eva burst out the door in a fury, and passed her daughter.

"Lela, what are you waiting for, come on!" she yelled.

Lela jumped up and ran to her mother's side. Eva's pace was so much swifter, Lela was having a hard time keeping up. As soon as they were safely across the street Eva turned towards her daughter and advised that she was to always be on her best behavior around her grandmother. Baffled by the request, she just nodded her head. She had no idea what she had done to upset her Grandma Eula, and why her mother was acting this way without explaining what she had done wrong.

Eva stormed away, leaving her daughter in the middle of the yard. Lela felt all alone; it was a familiar feeling she recognized. It was how she felt every time Eva visited her in Wewoka. The difference now was she didn't have Mama Grey to comfort her when her mother left. Did her mother want her, or not? What had just happened, and why hadn't her mother explained instead of just leaving her alone? Abandoned, she climbed into the bottom bunk and cried herself to sleep.

Lela's adjustment to life with her family proved to be both strenuous and exhausting. She didn't feel like she belonged. Her half-sisters had a bond, and she had a hard time relating to them. The resentment over the shared room lingered on both sides for the sisters. It was hard just to get through the week without fights and harsh words. To make the situation worse, every Sunday the entire family would have dinner at Grandmother Eula's. She did everything her mother told her to do to get in her good graces but failed. Lela started making up excuses for missing dinner, until eventually she just stopped going. Even though it was a relief to escape these horrible dinners, it also showed her again how she was separate from her family and didn't fit in. She was lonely in a house full of people. The only time Lela felt a connection with anyone was when her father was on leave from the military.

She cherished their time together. He always made her feel loved. "Daddy, can I come and live with you?" she asked.

"Honey, we have been through this before," he replied.

"Ok, can I go back and live with Mama Grey?" she asked.

"Lela, give it some time; you have only been here a few months. I am sure it will get better." Lela said nothing, but in her heart, she thought, *No, it won't.*

It broke his heart to hear Lela's desperate cries to leave her mother's care. If only Eva would stand up to her mother and exert her independence.

Lela packed her backpack carefully; she took her school books and hid them underneath her bed. She placed two pairs of dungarees along with one sweater in the bag. Lela quietly sneaked into the kitchen and fixed two peanut butter and jelly sandwiches. She placed them in a brown paper bag together with an apple. She then crawled into bed and waited until morning. Lela tossed and turned all night long; she had hoped her father would see her desperation to return to Mama Grey's house, but he didn't seem to care. She kept thinking about why Grandma Eula was so mean to her, and why did her mother just leave her in the middle of the yard? She thought, *I hate it here and I am never going to call Eva 'Mom'!*

The mornings were always a hectic time, everyone running around preparing for the day. "Good morning Lela, you're already ready?" her mom asked.

"Yes, ma'am," she replied.

"What's the hurry? School doesn't start for another hour and a half," Eva inquired.

"Oh, I am going to walk to school with a friend," she lied.

Eva thought that was odd. *Lela hasn't mentioned any friends.* She started to question her more but decided to let it go, so to avoid yet another fight. She was just glad Lela was making friends.

"Where are you heading to today?" the ticket agent asked.

"I am going to Wewoka," she replied.

"How many tickets do you need?" asked the agent.

"One, please," she replied.

"That will be $20.00."

Lela counted out exactly $20.00.

"Your bus will depart shortly from Pier Six."

Lela was hungry but decided to wait until she was safely on the bus. She didn't want to be distracted in case her mother came looking for her. She thought, *I can eat after the bus takes off. Where can I hide in case she does show up?* Lela sunk down as far as she could in her seat and didn't move until the bus almost left the station. Lela smiled at her accomplishment, but the real challenge would be to get Mama Grey to let her stay.

"Lela, is that you?" a familiar voice asked. The sun was shining so brightly, she could barely see the person. Using her hands to block the warm rays of the sun, she smiled when she saw it was Billy Ray. He was her father's best friend. They were inseparable as young boys and had planned to join the army together. However due to medical reasons Billy Ray was denied access into the army.

"Where are you headed, to Mama Grey's?" He answered his own question.

"Yes," she answered.

"Well come on, I'll give you a ride."

"Lela! Lord Jesus, thank you!" Mama Grey screamed when she saw her granddaughter getting out of Billy Ray's car. They ran into each other's arms. Mama Grey cupped Lela's face in her hands. "You ok baby? You hungry?" she asked.

"Yes, ma'am. Mama Grey, I don't want to go back there! Please, let me stay here. I promise, I won't be any trouble," Lela begged.

"We will talk later; right now go and wash up. I'll call you when dinner is ready," Mama Grey instructed.

Lela was so tired she slept through dinner. Mama Grey sat in the rocker and watched her grandbaby sleep. *Dear Lord, how do I tell my baby that she has to return to her mother? Give me the strength. Give me the words. Give me the courage.* She prayed.

The next morning at breakfast, Lela went on for hours about how horrific her life was in Oklahoma City. Mama Grey sat quietly as she vented.

"Lela, I don't know how to say this, but I guess just to say it. I can't keep you here. Your father is coming to get you. He will be here tomorrow. I tried reasoning with your parents, but your mother wants you home," Mama Grey said.

"Why? I don't understand why she wants me *now*? She didn't want me when I was a baby! All we do is fight, she doesn't defend me to Grandma Eula, who for some strange reason hates me. She doesn't talk to me. I hate them all!" she screamed as she ran out the door.

Against her better judgment, Eva let Lela stay with Mama Grey for a few days. When Lela returned home from the soda shop that afternoon, Mama Grey told her that her mother was allowing her to stay until Saturday. "Baby, you can't keep running here. First, it's not safe for you to be traveling alone. Second, you have to give your mother a chance. Now promise me you won't run away again."

"I promise." Lela knew the honor in her word and never ran away again. She thought, *as soon as I can, I will leave*.

When she arrived at the Oklahoma City bus depot, Eva was there waiting. Eva thought, *God, please help me reach my daughter. I know she is angry with me, and I will do everything in my power to correct my wrongs*. As soon as the bus pulled in, Eva jumped to her feet. She watched intently as each passenger off loaded. "Lela," she called out. Lela began walking in the direction of her mother's voice. "Oh baby, I am so glad you made it back safely." Eva leaned in to hug her daughter, but Lela stiffly rejected her mother's gesture.

They rode in strained silence most of the way home. Suddenly, Eva pulled the car over to speak with her daughter. "Lela, I know you're upset with me; you may even be angry, but I am your mother. And I can't have you just up and leave anytime you feel like it."

Eva remained silent for a while, hoping her daughter would engage in the conversation. "Lela, we have to work together. I am learning about you and hopefully you want to learn about me."

"Eva, why couldn't things stay the way they were? I mean, why couldn't I have stayed with Mama Grey?"

"Lela, it's complicated. I will explain one day. Meanwhile can we try to get along?"

Lela didn't respond for quite some time. She thought, *I have no one else to turn to. But if she thinks, I am going to call her Mom, she has another thing coming!* "Do you think I can have my own room?"

"Does that mean we are going to try to get along and no more running away?"

"Yes ma'am."

"Well, you got a deal. Can we shake on it?"

"Yes ma'am."

Eva was hoping for Mom but decided, *it's a start.*

"Why are you so excited, Lela?" Beverly asked.

Beverly King was Lela's only friend. While most of the other girls made fun of her because she was from the country, Beverly accepted Lela without judgement. She made her life in Oklahoma bearable.

"One more year and I'll be free. Free to move back to Wewoka and live with my granny," Lela said.

"A lot of things can happen in a year," Beverly said.

"You're right, I could meet my Prince Charming," Lela said. The girls burst out laughing and went to the registration table to get their class schedules.

"Look who is coming your way," Beverly said.

"Who?" Lela asked.

"Duke Baldwin, and he is checking you out."

"What would a boy like him want with someone like me?" she asked.

"Lela, who wouldn't want someone like you? You're very pretty. Why do you think those girls don't like you?" Beverly said.

Lela blushed. "Ok, who paid you to say those things?" Lela joked.

"Hey Lela," Duke said as he passed by.

"Be careful of that one, you know he has a reputation for being somewhat of a Casanova. A heart breaker. You know, the love them and leave them type of a guy!"

The bell rang and they separated and went to their respective classes.

When class was over Duke was standing in the hallway. He called out to her. She thought, *what is he doing here outside my classroom?* She quickly merged into the crowded hallway with the other students in an attempt to avoid Duke Baldwin. She began to slow down when she thought she was in the clear. Resting her forehead against the steel lockers, she heard someone ask her name. Lela nervously turned to see who was speaking to her.

"What is your name?" he asked

Baffled, she shrugged her shoulders and pointed at herself.

"Yes, I am talking to you," he said.

"Oh, my name is Lela," she shyly said.

"Are you new at Douglas High School?" he asked.

"Yes," she said. She thought, *what game is he playing? He just spoke to me the other day.*

"I thought so," he said as he lit a cigarette. "You want a drag?" He passed the cigarette to her.

"No, I don't smoke." She remembered the day he spied her watching him. When their eyes met, she took off running.

He caught up quickly; her scrawny legs were no match for his long muscular ones.

"Why were you staring at me?"

"I wasn't. Look, I have to get to class."

"Cool, I'll see you around."

Lela cautiously exited the classroom; the last thing she wanted was to run into Duke Baldwin. She took a long look down the corridor and he was nowhere in sight. Lela was happy the coast was clear, but she was also a little sad. Duke was the only boy who had shown any interest in her. She thought, *oh well he probably was just teasing me.*

Lela glanced at her watch and started to panic a bit. She had less than twenty minutes to get to her babysitting job at Ms. Jean Josephine's house. Lela liked sitting for Ms. Josephine but had to admit the lady scared her a bit. Ms. Josephine was a tall, stout woman with high cheekbones and a mouth like a drunken sailor. Lela thought, *I don't want to be her next victim or lose my job.* Lela was out of breath when she reached her front porch.

"Would you like some water?" a familiar voice asked.

"No thank you." When she looked up Duke was sitting on the porch. "What are *you* doing here!"

"Jean is my sister," he replied. Lela's mouth dropped open. She was dumbfounded by the news. "You must be the babysitter."

"Yes, I am, and I am late so move out of the way."

Seconds later, Ms. Josephine thrust open the door and started barking orders to Lela. Lela quickly went into the house and locked the door behind her. "Come on here boy and leave that girl alone, she's a good girl," she ordered.

"Aww Sis, I am a good guy," he winked.

"Jean, how long has she been watching the kids?"

"I don't know, maybe about a month or so. Why do you want to know? Duke, she is a nice country girl, don't start messing with her head with all your bull crap. Besides, the kids really like her, and I like her too! So, back off brother!"

"I guess I'll be stopping by more often," he mumbled.

"What did you say?"

"Nothing. I said nothing."

Ms. Jean would have her brother walk Lela home the nights she worked at the bar and Lela babysat her children. Lela didn't mind. She actually liked talking to him; besides, he was completely different when he was away from his friends. Other than Beverly, he was the only other student who talked to her.

Lela had just put the kids to bed when the phone rang. "Hello?"

"Lela this is Jean; I am sorry I am working late again tonight. I need you to stay there just a little bit longer. I have already spoken with your mother, and she has given her permission. My dad is coming by to sit with the kids until I get home and Duke will walk you home tonight."

"Yes ma'am." Lela was so happy she could barely contain her joy.

"Lela, my sister says she's sorry again for keeping you late on a school night and she hopes that your mother accepts her apology too. We hope your mom will understand, plus your sister has already called her as well."

They walked in silence for a few moments. Lela wanted to seem sophisticated, so she decided to break the ice. "What do you want to do when you graduate?" she asked.

"I don't know, probably work with my Pops at the shop," he replied.

"What about you?" he asked.

"I want to be an interior decorator," she proudly said.

"A what?"

"I have always wanted to be a professional decorator," she smiled.

"I like it when you smile, Lela. Most of the time you look so sad, why is that?" he inquired. Blushing, she looked down at the ground. "Hey pretty girl, look up," he said. Lela couldn't move. He gently raised her head until they were eye-to-eye. "What's the matter, did I say something wrong?" he asked.

Lela just shook her head *no*. Duke decided not to pressure her with more questions. Duke and Lela walked hand-in-hand the rest of the way.

"Mama Grey, I met the handsomest, most fantastic boy ever! His name is Duke! He goes to my school," she said. She thought it best that she didn't mention his age.

"I am glad to see you're making friends Lela, but I think you should focus on your schooling. You're only sixteen and you have your whole life to worry about boys. How old is this boy?"

"He goes to my school," Lela replied evasively. "I have to hang up now Mama Grey."

"Ok, baby." Lela hated lying to Mama Grey, but she knew if she remained on the phone longer, her Mama Grey would find out her secret.

Lela hadn't shared her secret with anyone, not even Beverly, her only true friend. How could she tell anyone that she gave her virginity to Duke? Lela thought, *out of all the people in the world, Mama Grey is the last person I want to disappoint.*

Beverly found her friend in the bathroom crying. "Hey Lela, why are you crying?" she asked.

"My friend didn't come this month."

"What? Are you sure?"

"Yes, I am sure," she sighed. Beverly hugged her friend.

"Did you check your calendar?"

"No, I am too afraid."

"Well, how have you been feeling?"

"Ok, I guess," she said. Lela shared with her best friend that she and Duke had gone all the way. "He told me he loves me!"

"They all say that. You know you have to tell him."

"I know." Lela wanted to share more with her friend but felt too ashamed and embarrassed. They stood in awkward silence until another student entered. "Well, we better get going to our next class. I'll talk with you later Lela." Beverly brushed closely by and touched her hand as she exited.

"I'll be out in a moment." Lela wanted to call her Granny and tell her before she heard it from someone else. But she didn't have the courage. She wished she had heeded her Granny's advice and concentrated on school. How could she explain to Mama Grey the loneliness she was feeling since she moved away? How could she deny her heart's love? Lela was so immersed in her thoughts that she missed the last bell for class and decided to skip the rest of her classes. Lela still had the daunting task of telling Duke; she hoped he would be happy.

She thought, *I might as well get this over with. I will tell him tomorrow.* The next day they planned to meet at their secret place. She just hoped he would be happy with the news.

As soon as she walked in, he started fondling her. "No, I didn't come here for that. Duke, I need to talk to you about something."

"We can talk later," he said.

"I am serious," she said.

"Ok, lay it on me," he said.

Lela hadn't really thought about how she was going to say it. She could sense he was getting restless. "Duke, I am pregnant with your baby," she said.

He jumped up so fast, it startled her. "What!" he exclaimed.

"I am pregnant," she repeated.

"Well, who is the father?"

Shocked, she slapped him across the face. "How dare you ask me that question," she said. Lela grabbed her jacket and high-tailed it out of there. Duke ran after her.

"Lela, come back. Stop! Wait a moment!" Lela slowed down so he could catch up with her.

"Lela, baby I'm sorry, I was wrong, forgive me." He reached for her hand as they walked back to his house. "I promise, I will be by your side."

Lela hid her pregnancy as best she could, but she was not able to fool Eva for long.

"Lela, are you pregnant?"

"Yes ma'am."

Eva was horrified. Her daughter had committed the same sin she had. What was Grandma Eula going to say? Eva knew she would be facing her mother's wrath once again and would hear what a horrible sinner Eva was. She also knew that Eula was going to lash out at her, condemn her for her own unwed pregnancy, and double her punishment on Eva for her granddaughter's sin.

"What were you thinking? Oh, wait, you obviously weren't thinking! What kind of slut are you? You are a disgrace to our family." Even as Eva lashed out at her daughter, she refused to think about how she had felt as a young unmarried, pregnant woman, and how badly she had wanted her mother Eula to comfort her, not attack her. But even knowing this, Eva was helpless to stop attacking her daughter.

"Okay, well, you have made your bed, and now you are going to lie in it. You are going to tell your Grandma Eula the sin you have brought upon our family, and Grandma Eula will tell you what you are going to do."

"Eva, please, come with me."

Eva thought, *even now she doesn't call me Mom, but she still wants my support.*

Ungrateful child. Well, let's see how she feels when Grandma Eula is done with her.

With that, Eva marched Lela over to Grandmother Eula. Lela could see her mother's disappointment, and was ashamed for herself, but sensed there was something deeper Eva was concealing. Lela searched her mother's angry face, but she yielded no answers. Eva opened the door and led her daughter to the wolf.

She could hear the faintest sounds of a clock; *tick-tock, tick-tock, tick-tock.* With each step she took the rhythmic sound grew louder. She sensed her time of judgment was rapidly approaching. She moved through the sterile living area where everything was covered in plastic slipcovers to protect the furniture from being soiled. Lela thought, *who would protect her heart from being stained and tarnished?*

She continued through the house until she reached the doorway of Grandma Eula's room. Even though she had a beautiful house, Eula resided in the cold, musty basement. Despite the continuous playing of gospel music, the room had a dark and evil presence. In every corner of the room was some type of religious artifact just waiting to condemn her very existence. Lela had to descend three steep steps to enter into Eula's sanctuary. These steps would lead her into the den of fire and brimstone, where she would be judged and persecuted for her sins.

As she took the first step, she thought of her mother's persecution and how she had been ridiculed and made to feel shameful. When Lela took the second step, she questioned why her mother did not save her from this inquisition. And why would Eva make her re-live her persecution with her Grandma Eula? Wasn't it enough to be condemned by her mother? By the third step she was fully immersed in her persecution and had accepted her place in the family as the cursed seed.

Lela stood in silence with her head bowed down, waiting for her Grandma Eula's interrogation. With the quickness of a poisonous snake, her venomous tongue, Eula began her mental thrashing that struck at the core of Lela's fragile foundation. She was told that she would never amount to anything, nor would her bastard child. And all she would be good for was lying on her back. She reiterated that like her mother, she had brought shame and disgrace to the family. Lela noted that but didn't understand. How had her mother brought shame and disgrace to the family? The verbal insult went on for what seemed like an eternity and at times she didn't even know what Eula was spitting out because she was focused on the lack of movement of her unborn child.

When Lela was released from Eula's bondage, she started to ascend from the pit of hell. Clutching her belly, she vowed to prove Eula wrong. Her child would amount to something, and she would complete high school. Lela also made a sacred promise to her unborn child that he or she would never experience shame or abandonment.

Eula demanded that Lela must save the family from shame because of her indiscretion and marry the father of her child. When she emerged from the pit of hell, she found Eva at the top. She called out to her, but her cries fell on deaf ears. Eva just stood there in a zombie-like trance, staring down into Grandma Eula's s room. Lela pushed past her mother and made her way to her grandma's living room couch.

Lela searched Eva's eyes, looking for a reason why her mother would allow Grandma Eula to berate her. After what seemed like a lifetime, Eva finally spoke.

Eva broke her silence. "What did your grandma say?" she asked.

Lela looked baffled; she didn't understand why her mother was concerned with what Grandma Eula desired. "Why do you care?" Lela refused to answer and stormed out.

Lela called her dad when she reached her mother's house. Sadly, he was not available. Lela made several attempts, but all were unsuccessful. Just before she went to bed, Eva knocked on her door. She pretended she was asleep, but Eva proceeded with her message.

"Lela, I called your father, and he will be here this weekend," Eva said.

Lela woke up early Saturday morning to prepare for her dad's visit. She wanted to look her best, so she took extra care with her grooming. She picked out her best dress and curled her locks. When she walked into the living room, she found her parents huddled up.

Eva left the room. Lela fell into her dad's arms; she began to cry immediately. Before she could utter a word, he softly stroked her head and whispered that he knew. Fox held onto his baby girl until her weeping ceased. Lela gently pulled away from her dad's arms and began to share with him the horrific scene that occurred in Grandma Eula's basement.

"Dad, she demanded that I marry Duke. I don't want to get married Dad."

Fox pulled her closer to him and held her tight. "Baby girl, you don't have to marry him," Fox said.

Later that day, Lela overheard her parents discussing Eula.

"Eva, we are going to support Lela in her decision," he said.

"Will you be here with me Fox?" she asked.

"I can't be here, the Army is shipping me overseas," he said. "Eva, not too long ago we were forced to marry; don't you remember how miserable we were and the hardship of trying to survive?" he said. Lela stood outside the door. *Her parents had been forced to marry due to an unplanned pregnancy?*

Eva timidly agreed with her husband and said she would support their daughter in her decision. Eva agreed to go and speak with her mother the following day. Fox had entrusted this task with Eva because he was due back to the military base. As the day progressed, Eva felt her courage diminishing with each passing hour. She didn't have the courage or the strength to stand against her mother and by day's end she had succumbed to her fears and left Lela's fate in the hands of her mother.

Eva reasoned with herself, believing that she could have confronted Eula if Fox had remained in town, but without his support she was powerless to stand against her mother. Furthermore, Eva thought it had taken her years to get back in favor with Eula and the thought of disobeying her wishes was out of the question. Eva's final thoughts on the matter were that they would do as Eula stipulated.

When Lela's father left, Eula saw her opportunity to put her plan into place. She knew her wishes would prevail because Eva was not strong enough to override her. However, on her initial attempt Duke refused to marry Lela. Lela was ecstatic and thought her prayers had been answered, but Eula had another card up her sleeve.

The next day, Eula went to Duke's parents and threatened to put him in jail if he didn't marry Lela, since she was a minor. In her father's absence there was not a soul to fight for Lela, so at the age of sixteen she was pregnant and engaged to marry.

Lela walked out of the bride's waiting room adorned in her mother's oversized wedding dress. Although it was too large for her small frame, it was the perfect size to hide her rapidly growing belly. The bridal march commenced; Lela began the long treacherous march down to the altar. With each step her breath became shallower, and her legs felt limp, like wet noodles.

The words *lie and deceit* ran through her mind like a ticker tape. As she surveyed her guests, she noticed some were weeping, while others held contemptuous looks upon their faces. Lela grasped her grandfather's hand as tightly as she could, never wanting to let go. Sensing his granddaughter's anxiety, Elijah leaned in slightly and whispered "Buttercup, God never gives us more than we can handle."

Lela smiled at her grandfather's attempt to comfort her and thought *God does not care about those who have sinned against him and was certain this forced marriage was His* way *of interceding on her behalf and saving her soul.*

Once they reached the altar, the pastor asked, "Who gives this woman to be married to this man?"

Elijah replied, "I do."

Elijah kissed his granddaughter and reluctantly walked to his seat. The pastor asked everyone to bow their heads for prayer. Lela couldn't concentrate on what the pastor was saying. Her mind was racing with thoughts of her father bursting into the church and saving her. It wasn't until she heard the pastor clearing his throat that she realized that she had drifted off.

The pastor jokingly said, "Now that we are all present, Lela, do you take Duke for your lawfully wedded husband?"

Lela glanced over her shoulder in hope, but to no avail. Her father would not save her today. Lela slowly turned and faced Duke and softly said, "I do."

In unison the entire church let out a sigh of relief. Not wanting to delay the ceremony any longer, the pastor swiftly turned to the groom and repeated the vows. Duke quickly answered and with a ceremonial kiss the couple was pronounced husband and wife.

They were showered with a streaming flow of white rice as they exited the church. Just beyond the last step awaited their chariot, Duke's dad's 1959 "Old Daddy" Ford pick-up truck. On the back of the old tarnished bumper was an array of tin cans and bottles, together with streamers and ribbons. Fixed to the trunk door was a sign with the words *Just Married.*

Lela had ridden in the truck on many occasions but had never noticed how corroded it was. She thought, *what happened during the life of the truck; what happened to the shine and lustre of the car?* All that was visible was the harsh life its owner had imposed on it.

Lela glanced over at Duke and thought *what toll would this loveless marriage take on her life?* With Duke's help, she stepped up into the truck and carefully sat on the faded, tattered vinyl seat. Duke climbed in behind the oversized steering wheel, turned on the engine and they drove off in silence to their new life.

The young couple took up residence in Duke's parents' home. Lela had always admired his parents' home; it was nestled between pecan and fruit trees. There were always squirrels running about. It was tiny in comparison to Grandma Eula's house, but charming in its own way. From the front yard no one would ever imagine that the house was set on a slope. Just beyond the backyard was a hill perfect for snow sledging in the winter.

Duke opened the door to their new home. His bedroom was located in the back of the house. The room was filthy! There were dirty clothes everywhere. Empty food containers were stacked on the windowsill. Lela had been in his room before but didn't recall it being this messy.

Lela said, "It looks like a tornado has been through here!"

Duke snottily replied, "You didn't seem to mind before."

They both blushed at the thought of the first time they had sex in his room.

Duke's parents were polite to Lela when they were together. But when they were apart Mrs. Baldwin showed Lela how much she loathed her. As far as Mrs. Baldwin was concerned, it was Lela's fault that she was pregnant. Lela quickly learned how to maneuver through the house in order to avoid her. Their only source of income was Duke's part-time job as a grocery bagger. Lela was still attending school—something she was determined to complete, which left the couple very dependent on their families. Lela hated being in this situation, but to her surprise it didn't seem to bother her husband.

Lela sat quietly in the living room listening to the wood burning in the fireplace. The crackling, hissing, and popping noises were music to her ears. The sounds briefly took her mind off of her problems. Through school acquaintances, Lela learned of rumours of Duke cheating. And since he was never home, even when he was not working, she believed them to be true. The infidelity, coupled with the anxiety of being two-weeks past her due date, left her fearful of her marriage. Lela shrugged her shoulders and took a long, deep breath.

Feeling restless, Lela clumsily lifted herself off the sofa and walked over to the window. It was a greyish, chilly day. She began stroking her belly as she spoke to her unborn child.

"I am eager to meet you! Don't you want to meet me?" Lela paused, not really sure what she was expecting to happen. Laughing at herself she thought, *how silly it was that she was waiting for a response.*

It felt good to laugh, even if it was at herself. As she made her way back to the sofa, she suddenly felt liquid running down her legs! A swarm of emotions flooded her thoughts, but the one clear message was that her baby was just as eager to be born as she was ready to meet him or her.

"Mama Baldwin, help! I think the baby is coming!" *Of all people here with me today, it would be his mama! Baby, couldn't you have waited until your father get home!* She yelled out again, "Mama Baldwin, the baby is coming!"

"I heard you the first time, I am getting your bag! Ok, I got your bag and I have called the doctor and Duke and his father are on their way to the hospital!" Lela thought, *why couldn't she had said that instead of ignoring me!*

"Push sweetheart push, we are almost there," the nurse commanded.

Lela grabbed onto the metal railings and sucked in as much air as her lungs could hold. Lela begun to push with all her might until sweat dripped from her forehead and at the release of that breath, the baby's head crowned.

"Lela, you're doing great my dear, we just need one more good push and you will be holding your baby!" said the nurse.

Breathless, Lela just gave an assuring nod and prepped her body into position. On the nurse's order, Lela bellowed out the most unique cry unto the world as she felt her baby being released from her womb!

"It's a girl! You have a healthy baby girl," said the nurse.

Moments later the nurse laid the baby across her shoulder and a floodgate of emotions took over. Through her tears all she could see was her baby's jet-black locks. Her hair swallowed her face. Lela looked into her baby's face and promised that she would never feel alone. Lela promised to always protect her. Lela also thought that *she* would never be alone again, that she would always have someone to love. Daniela Grace Baldwin had entered this world.

BOOK IV

Daniela Grace Baldwin's Story

Daniela Grace Baldwin-Wondering Butterfly Age: 6-14

One of my earliest childhood memories is the day I sat carefree near my Great-Grandmother Eula's flower bed watching the clouds slowly move across the sky. Their leisurely pace gave me just enough time to guess what picture they were forming. I particularly liked the big, "fat", fluffy ones. I imagined them carrying me far away to different lands and adventures. I was so immersed in my thoughts that I missed my turn at being the imaginary light post in the game "red light, green light." I leapt up to join in, but when I looked around no one had noticed my absence. So I shrugged my shoulders and continued to watch the parade in the sky.

I spent many of my days mesmerized by Mother Nature's beauty. I delighted in the continuous flow of the seasons. Spring was my favorite. The winter's color scheme of brown hues would fade away, making room for a multitude of colors representing every facet of the rainbow. The blooming flowers alerted the butterflies of their readiness to share their nectar. The gentle shoving of the mother bird, giving signals to her chicks to spread their wings for flight.

I thought, *everything in nature seems to know its reason for being.* I couldn't help but wonder what my purpose was. I was painfully shy as a child. Communication outside of my immediate family was a rarity. There were many times I desperately wanted to join in conversations, but my vocal cords always held my tongue hostage. However, there was one person who was able to free me from my silent bondage, my Great-Grandma Maikoda.

Great-Grandma Maikoda was the mother of my dad's father. She was the direct bloodline to my Indian heritage. She had long shiny-silver hair that she kept swept up in a bun. Deeply rooted wrinkles ran across her forehead, and she had slightly sunken eyes that were as bright as the sun. It was through her stories that I learned to respect every creature, season, and the wisdom of the Earth. I would escape to her tiny house that was perched on top of a mountain---at least that's what it felt like to my tiny legs, as often as I could.

It was the first day of summer and I was so excited. I woke early and did my chores and headed straight away to my Great-Grandmother Maikoda's house. "Hello Great-Grandma Mai," I said, as I ran into her open arms.

"What is my name, child?' she replied.

"It's Great-Grandma Maikoda, but why do other people just call you Mai?" I asked.

"Because most folks cannot properly pronounce my name and it pains me so to hear them butcher it up," she chuckled. "Besides, my great-grandmother took great pride in choosing my name. Would you like to hear the story?" she asked.

I nodded my head excitedly.

"Dani, your ancestors are from the Seminole Indian tribe. In our tradition the women name the children on the second rising of the full moon after birth. On the night of my naming ceremony, because your great-grandmother could see the moon's full reflection in my eyes, she named me Maikoda, which means *the moon is powerful*."

"What does it mean *the moon is powerful*?" I asked.

"I don't rightly know for sure, but I have come to understand that the moon has power over the Earth." She paused, then continued, "I guess in due time it will be revealed to me."

"Great-Grandma Maikoda," I asked, "What does my name mean?"

She replied, "I don't know, child."

Sadly, I bowed my head down. "I want my name to mean something too," I whined.

"Don't worry child, Great-Grandma will give you a great Indian name, that has character and definition," she said.

"When?" I asked.

"On the rise of the next full moon," she replied. "The traditions of our people are being lost. Folks are just making up names that have no significant values. But don't you fret child, Great-Grandma will take care it," she passionately ranted.

The sky is illuminating a cascade of blue tones; Mother Earth is pleased today. This will be a great day to ponder a name for my dear great-granddaughter, Great-Grandma Maikoda thought. The oak leaves were gently swaying in the wind. They called to her to come and rest from the warmth of the sun. Accepting the invitation, she kneeled and took refuge under the foliage of her host. She asked the heavens for a name that would inspire Dani to come out of her shell. She longed for her to be as expressive and openhearted with others as she was with her. She thought, *what name would inspire her great-granddaughter so that the world could witness the beauty of her spirit?*

Just then a monarch butterfly came fluttering by. Maikoda carefully watched as the butterfly traveled from flower to flower, extracting their nectar. Inspired by the grace and beauty of the butterfly she chose the name "Wondering Butterfly" for her great-granddaughter.

I emerged from my bath excited with anticipation. I wondered what name Great-Grandma Maikoda would bless me with. I grabbed the oversized bath towel and wrapped it around my shivering body. It was so soft and fluffy—I imagined the clouds must feel like this. I slid into my slippers and headed into the bedroom.

Laid across Great-Grandma Maikoda's bed was a white dress with an alluring headband next to it. On her vanity table I found my great-grandma's favorite hairbrush. I picked it up and started to mimic her strokes. After dressing, I turned towards the dressing mirror and smiled at my reflection.

"Dani, are you ready?" my Great-Grandma called.

"Yes, I'm coming," I replied.

I was greeted by a cool breeze as I descended the back-porch steps. The backyard had been transformed into a festival of lights. Even the heavenly stars seemed to be hung lower and brighter. I followed the rhythmic beating of the drum down the lighted pathway to the grand old oak, where I found Great-Grandma Maikoda waiting. Great-Grandma was dressed in a buckskin Indian dress with beaded moccasins and leggings. Her silver locks were plaited into two long braids, with an elaborate hand-dressing resting on top. She looked so regal I curtsied. Resting on the ground behind Great-Grandma Maikoda was a white box with a blood-orange ribbon.

Great-Grandma Maikoda motioned for me to join her under the oak. She tenderly cleared my hair away from my brows, kissed my forehead and whispered, "Are you ready?" I nodded.

From her satchel she removed a ceremonial blanket. "Daniela Grace, this blanket has been passed down from generation to generation by the women of our family. One day, I will pass it on to you," she said.

Great-Grandma started unfolding the blanket in a reverent, ceremonious manner. She laid it on the ground and asked me to kneel down. Great-Grandma opened her arms toward the heavens and began to pray. She asked God to send angels to protect me and keep me safely out of harm's way.

I found it hard to focus as she prayed. My curiosity kept my mind fixed on the white box. I imagined the box contained a secret treasure map that would take me on an adventurous quest. The beating of the drum interrupted my thoughts and brought me back to the present moment.

Looking toward the moonlit sky, Great-Grandma Maikoda said "I present to you *Wondering Butterfly*."

I repeated the words *Wondering Butterfly* once out loud and then several times to myself. With tears glistening down my cheeks, I nodded with approval. To complete the ritual Great-Grandma Maikoda presented the white box to me. I eagerly opened it and found a silver bracelet embedded with four turquoise butterfly stones. Each stone was unique. I tenderly rubbed my fingers across each stone.

"Oh, Great-Grandma Maikoda I love it, I am never going to take it off. Thank you!" I said.

"You are welcome, child," she said.

We sat underneath the stars eating sweet bread and drinking Great-Grandma's Maikoda special elderberry tea until my belly was full.

"Great-Grandma Maikoda, why *Wondering Butterfly*, and what does it mean?" I asked.

"My child, I chose the name because that is how I see you."
I sat, listening intently as she paused. "Do you know what the
word *wondering* implies?"

"No, Great-Grandma, I am not exactly sure," I said.

"Well would you say you're curious, Daniela?" Great-
Grandma asked.

I nodded my head.

"Would you say you're a great listener and thinker?"

I nodded again. Suddenly, I thought of my favorite book
"Curious George" and how that silly monkey was always
getting into trouble.

"Daniela, you are inquisitive about the world and all that it
has to offer. This is one of the reasons I chose the word *Wondering*.
Now would you like to know why I selected the word *butterfly*?"
Great-Grandma said.

"Oh yes, Great-Grandma. I love butterflies," I said.

"Daniela, butterflies go through several stages before they
become the remarkable creature so many admire. The process
is called metamorphosis."

I gave Great-Grandma a perplexed look. "Meta-whatphosis?"

Great-Grandma smiled. "You see Dani, in their first stage as
caterpillars they crawl from leaf to leaf, eating until their bellies
are full. You would think that they didn't have a care in the world.
But they do. You see Daniela, they are taking it all in," she stated.

"Taking in what?" I asked.

"They are assessing what their world will be like when they
emerge as butterflies. For some this will be an easy transition,
but others may have difficulties adjusting."

"What would they have to worry about, Great-Grandma?" I asked.

"Daniela, within our world co-exist many other worlds. For example, there is the animal and plant world and some of their concerns could be the pollution of water and air."

"Ok, so what happens next, Great-Grandma?" I asked.

"Well, the next phase is a very important. It is the cocoon stage; it's where the butterfly is preparing for its grand appearance. The butterfly is wrapped in unconditional love, which gives it the strength and courage to deal with the struggles of the world. It is here where it learns the secret of life. The secret is Self-Love."

Great-Grandma stopped speaking and rested her eyes on me. I just looked into my great-grandma's eyes. I knew she had said something very profound and some of it made sense, but most of it was confusing.

Great-Grandma placed her hand under my chin and gently lifted my head and said, "All you ever need is within you. You have the same strength and courage of a butterfly. When you feel lost and confused remember these words."

We walked slowly back to the house. When we reached the back door, I flung my arms around my great-grandma, never wanting to let go. "Great-Grandma, I wish it could be like this forever and always. Just me and you picking the herbs and making the medicine. I love you Great-Grandma."

" I love you too."

They held onto each other a little longer. "One last thing Sweetie. Remember, *everything you will ever need is within you*, and I will always be with you too.

"Now, it's been a long night *Wondering Butterfly*, off to bed you go," she said.

Yes ma'am," I replied.

A year later…

"Dani, come here," my mom called.

"I'm coming," I replied. The moment I entered the room an eerie feeling came over me.

"Dani, come and sit down." She patted the space next to her. "There is no easy way to say this. Mai…"

I interrupted her and said "Maikoda has she passed?"

"Yes, you're right. Maikoda has passed on."

"No," I screamed, "That's not true! She wouldn't leave me!"

What my mother said after that was a blur. I turned and ran out of the house as fast as I could. I had to see for myself. I burst into my great-grandmother's house; people were everywhere, but only the elders were seated. Pastor Cornelius was standing in the center of the room, consoling with words of comfort.

"She has gone to meet her Maker and she is in a much better place," he said. I slid past the adults and dashed into her room. The curtains had been drawn, making it difficult for me to see.

"Great-Grandma Maikoda," I called out as I maneuvered through the darkness. I didn't realize there was someone already in the room.

"Your Great-Grandma Mai has gone to a better place." Startled, I thought I was alone, I pushed past the shadowed person and ran out the back door. I didn't stop until I reached the oak tree. Nestled under the oak— Great-Grandma's favorite place—I found my voice to release my pain. "Great-Grandma, why did you leave me?" I repeatedly cried out.

"Daniela, your great-grandma is still with you," a familiar voice said. I looked up to find my great-grandfather Papa standing above me.

"Where, Papa?" I asked.

"Daniela, your grandma lives within you through your memories, and she is always with you," Papa said.

"How can that be, Papa? I can't see or touch her," she said.

"Dani, although we aren't able to physical see or touch her, she lives on in our hearts. If we listen carefully to the whistling of the wind, the motion of the leaves, and the rising of the moon, we will find her. Now come, let us pay our respects."

Papa took his great-granddaughter by the hand and guided her to the family limousine. Daniela rested her head against her great-grandfather's shoulders and softly closed her eyes.

"Dani, wake up; it's time to go in," she heard her mother say.

"Ok, where is Papa?" she asked.

"He has to take care of things child; you will see him inside."

Not a smidgen of life was present anywhere in the sunless sanctuary. The agonizing moans and groans of the mourners filled the room. Ushers were hurrying about fanning the distraught guests and family members. I thought, *Pastor Cornelius said her passing on wasn't a sad occasion and we would celebrate her life today. Then why wasn't anyone celebrating her life, and why was there such sadness?*

We joined the slow-moving procession of mourners to pay our final respects. I clutched Papa's hand and peered into the casket, but found no signs of Great-Grandma, other than her physical body. Silently, I called out, *Where are you, Great-Grandma?*

"Ashes to ashes, dust to dust," Pastor Cornelius started reciting as they released Great-Grandma Maikoda back to Earth. I refused to believe my great-grandma was going into the dark, cold ground. I called again, "Great-Grandma, where are you?"

When we arrived home, I ran to my room. I could hear my mother calling me to come and eat but I ignored her. I heard my Grandma Madeline say, "Let the child rest, she'll come down when she gets hungry."

Awakened by my own self-inflicted tussling, I found myself at the foot of my bed. In a drunken stupor, I rose to my feet, and moved toward the light of the moon. Immediately a familiar sense of warmth and love filled my soul. I rested in this moment for a while. "Goodnight Great-Grandma Maikoda," I whispered.

2 years later...

"Papa, put that child down," Grandma Madeline hollered from the kitchen window.

"No," I whispered in his ear, "Keep going Papa; I can almost reach them."

Papa stood as sturdy as a Sequoia tree. His broad shoulders served as a perfect seat for star gazing. "Ok, get ready; one, two, three and up you go," Papa said.

"I got it Papa," I exclaimed as I pretended to pull a star from the heavens.

"What in tarnation are you two doing?" Grandma Madeline asked.

"Grandma, I just picked the most beautiful star from the sky. Do you want to see it?" I asked.

"Of course I do," Grandma said. Papa sat down on the back porch so I could climb down. I walked cautiously toward Grandma. I carefully opened my tiny hand so she could view my treasure.

"Look Grandma, isn't it the most beautiful star you've ever seen?"

"Yes, it is and a bright one too," she warmly said. "Daniela, you know what must be done now," Grandma said.

"No," I replied.

"You must release it back," she said.

I cleverly said, "Grandma, it is just one star out of millions. It surely will not be missed." Grandma just smiled and patted me on the head.

"Papa, I think tonight is a good night to tell her," Grandma said as she walked away.

"Come sit next to Papa," he said. I snuggled in. We sat silently for a while observing the constellation. "Dani, you know your grandma is right about letting go of the star. The stars, like much of nature, belong to everyone to admire and praise. They are a gift from God. You know Dani, if you were able to keep a star, eventually the magic would start to fade," Papa said.

"Papa I would take great care of my star."

"I know you would Baby, but stars have a much greater purpose."

"Papa, I don't understand."

"I know you don't understand completely but one day you will, Wondering Butterfly." I smiled. I hadn't been called Wondering Butterfly since my Great Grandma Maikoda passed.

"Baby girl, make a wish and send it home among the other stars and it will always be there watching over you just like Great-Grandma Maikoda." I made my wish and released my star. "Daniela, one day Grandma and Papa will leave this Earth, and just like your star we will always be here for you," Papa said.

"No, Papa, I am never leaving you," I said. Papa kissed me on the top of my head and sent me off to bed.

"Garthard, did you tell Dani?" my grandmother asked.

"I told her as best I could. I just wish Lela would stay here, so we can help her with the kids."

"I know, me too," Madeline said. "Are you coming to bed?"

"I'll be up later." Feeling restless, Papa sat down in his rocker on the back porch. He kept wishing there was a way to convince Lela to stay, but he knew she was stubborn and tired of dealing with his son. Out of all of his grandchildren it was Dani that he worried about the most. He thought, *it's been just a little over two years since the passing of Maikoda and that loss had been devastating on Dani, so much so she isolated herself from everyone, not allowing anyone in. Now with Lela uprooting her from the only home she has ever know, I fear she will climb back into her shell.* Feeling the soft touch of his wife's hand brought him back to the present.

"Come to be bed dear." Papa got up and followed Madeline.

"Mama, I don't want to go to a new house, I want to stay here with Grandma and Papa," I said. She briefly stopped packing.

"You don't have a choice Daniela, now go and check on your brother and sister." I couldn't move. I stood motionless, watching her throw our lives into those empty cardboard boxes.

"Where are we going?" I asked.

"Far away from here. Now go do as I asked!" she replied.

Defeated, I lowered my head. I thought, *my world is falling apart. Everyone that loves me is deserting me.* As the mountain of boxes disappeared from Papa's house, I realized life as I knew it would soon vanish too.

"Well Lela, that's the last of it. You know we don't mind keeping the kids this weekend," Papa said.

"I know, Papa. This is hard on everyone, especially Dani. I'm afraid delaying it—even by one day, will give her false hopes."

"I really wish you would stay here with the kids," Papa said.

"I can't stay here with your son any longer. Papa, you have been more of a father to our children than he has. I appreciate everything you and Madeline have done for us. Please try to understand."

"Dani, it's time to go. Gather your things and get in the car," Lela said. I refused to answer. "Daniela Grace, I know you hear me!" she yelled.

"Lela, be patient with the child. This is the only home she has ever known. I'll go and get her," Madeline said. Lela nodded politely out of respect, but deep inside she believed her mother-in-law was partially to blame for the demise of their marriage. She was always taking his side even when he was clearly in the wrong. She thought, *I've got to get the hell out of here!*

"Dani, come and sit with Papa in the truck," he asked.

With my arms folded and my fists clutched, I said, "I am ok here Papa." I watched as my siblings kissed Papa goodbye. I desperately wanted to join them, but my anger held me back.

"Dani, stop acting like a child and go kiss your Papa goodbye," Lela said.

Running, I yelled out, "Papa wait!" I jumped into his arms. "Please take me with you," I whispered. I held my breath in anticipation.

"Be a good girl and help your mother," is all he said before walking away.

"Goodbye Papa," I said.

From the first day we moved into this tiny house, I hated it. Two months later, I loathed it even more. With only two bedrooms and one bath for all of us to share, our apartment made my former home look like a castle. To make matters worse, I could no longer display my cherished things, especially the ones from Great-Grandma Maikoda.

There was simply no breathing room, and Mom didn't help the situation, as she wouldn't allow us to go outside and play with the other kids. From day to night, we were trapped inside that tiny sweat box. Our only reprieve was when Papa came to our rescue and took us back to his home. And because it was summer, Papa was usually able to talk Mom into letting us stay for a week.

"Dani, get the breakfast on the table. Go and check on your sister and brothers, make sure they are up and ready," her mother ordered.

"Yes, ma'am," I answered. It was during moments like this I really missed my grandparents. Not only did I have to adjust to my new life and surroundings, I had to learn how to balance all the adult responsibilities thrust upon me. I was responsible for caring for my siblings as well as my mother, instead of enjoying childhood. I longed for the days in the past when I could escape to Great-Grandma Maikoda.

I woke up to the musical sound of B.B King. I knew my mother was feeling sad and lonely. I lay awake, like a watchful mother bird. I imagined her slumped over the stereo, singing along with the artist.

"Wake up Daniela," I faintly heard my mother say.

I shifted about a bit and mumbled "Ok, I'm up."

So I wouldn't disturb my siblings, I grabbed my slippers and robe and dressed in the hallway. I followed her into the living room. We stood in an awkward silence. Scared, I found comfort in the humming sounds of the refrigerator. My thoughts were running rapidly. *Why had she awakened me and why is she just standing there? I knew what to do when she played her music, but this was different, and I am scared.*

Perhaps sensing my anxiety, she began to speak. Her voice was dry and lifeless. "Daniela, I am going out for food. Lock the door behind me and don't open it for anyone," she said. Perplexed and powerless to do anything, I just nodded. As she reached for the doorknob, she abruptly stopped and took a step backward. For a brief moment I thought the madness was over. She went into the kitchen and swiftly grabbed something from the cutlery drawer. I spied as best I could, but she quickly concealed her quest.

I locked the door and ran to the window. I closely scrutinized her body movements. Her shoulders were squared. Her arms and legs moved in perfect synchronized unison, like a military troop headed off to battle. My heart started beating uncontrollably as her silhouette faded into the darkness. I sat by the window, too afraid to move an inch.

I thought, *why did she need a knife to get food, and what would I do if she didn't return? Who would take us in and why did she keep us so isolated?* Restless and exhausted, I decided to lay down underneath the window and wait for her return. I fought like hell to keep my eyes open. But the magnitude of the situation was too much for me to bear, and I succumbed to the peace of sleep.

Dreams found me. I opened my eyes to a vortex of colors across the horizon. Large black berries dripping with dew enticed me. As I reached for them the heavens darkened. I turned around to find a furious canine barreling towards me. I started running for my life. In the midst of my nightmare, I started hearing whispers summoning me to awaken. I raised my head to get a view of the messenger but was blinded by the light streaming through the window. I squinted to get a clearer view.

Excitedly, I leapt up! "Mom, you're home?" I asked.

"Yes, now go to bed. Dani, go to bed," she ordered.

Dear God, I promise to be a good helper and take care of my mother and siblings. God, thank you for returning her home safely. God, could you make it possible for her not to leave us again?

Exhausted from a hard day of playing, we scurried about picking up our mess—as our mother would say, before she arrived. Click-clack went the lock tumblers. I scanned the area, and everything seemed to be in order. My younger brother ran to the door to greet her but ran back into my arms when he saw something in her shadow.

"Hello, kids," she said. Not a word was uttered by us. There was a stranger standing with her. We were all taken aback. One by one, she introduced us. "This is Mr. Morehouse."

"Hello," we replied unanimously.

"Hi kids," he replied in a commanding voice. Every facial feature was chiseled in perfect proportion to his thick mustache. My scrutiny of the strange-looking man with the commanding voice was interrupted by my mother's overwhelming excitement. I turned toward my siblings for clarification, but they were just as baffled as I was.

Mr. Morehouse, noticing our confusion, jumped in and added more information. In a falsetto positive voice he said "Guess what, kids? Me and your mother are getting married, and we all are going to live in Hawai'i!"

My siblings and I huddled in even closer. I thought, *who the hell are you and why are you here?* My mother abruptly interrupted my thoughts.

"What do you think, Dani?" my mother chimed in.

How could I say what I really felt when she was beaming with excitement? I was screaming *No!* on the inside, *please don't do this again! Don't introduce us to another man who is going to break your heart and ours too!* But instead I told her what she wanted to hear.

"It's good news Mom," I said. I looked toward Mr. Morehouse and when our eyes met, I could see that he was just as scared as we were. I thought, *what convinced him to take on the challenge of a mother with four children.* I pondered the question for a moment or so; and when no answer was revealed, I shrugged my shoulders and embraced the idea of living in Hawai'i. Plus, I was curious about this funny-looking man with the distinctive voice.

Mom and Mr. Morehouse were married in a private ceremony at the county courthouse.

"Com'on kids, get in the car," Mr. Morehouse instructed. We were going to Ft. Sill military base. I was excited; I thought it would give me an idea of what my new life might entail. Everywhere we turned there was the rhythmic sounds of soldiers marching. *Hut, two, three four,* they sang as they marched in perfect sync.

I quickly became discouraged with life on a military base; the compound was lifeless in color. Multiple shades of browns and green as far as one could see. Only patches of grass peeked through the ground. The buildings and housing followed suit. This was not what I imagined Hawai'i was going to look like.

"Mr. Morehouse, will we live in a house like those?" I asked.

"No Dani, these units house the soldiers. We will live a home much like your grandmother's," he said. Relieved, I sat back and listened to the pulsating sounds of the marching men and women.

I couldn't sleep. I had lain awake all night, trying to imagine what it would feel like to fly on a plane. I couldn't imagine floating around in the sky. When Mom came to wake us, I was already dressed and completely packed. I watched as Mr. Morehouse maneuvered through the busy traffic. I had never seen so many yellow cabs, honking and bullying their way ahead of us. A man with rolling carts approached our car as we pulled up. I watched the man load our bags onto his cart within a matter of minutes. He placed tags on our bags. Mr. Morehouse gave the man a wad of money and he in return gave him some paper receipts.

"Where is he taking our bags?"

"Dani, he is a porter, he works for the airline, and he is taking our bags to the plane." I walked slowly behind my family. I wanted to take in everything.

"Ok kids, we are at our gate. Do not wander too far," Mr. Morehouse instructed.

There was a commotion by the window. I was curious, so I headed toward the excitement. As I made my way to the front of the crowd, I could have never imagined that an airplane would be so large. Awestruck, I stood in amazement with the other passengers looking at the airplane. It was huge, the biggest contraption I had ever seen! I watched busy workers loading metal containers. There were trucks with hidden jacks and hoses swarming around. I thought *how is something this massive going to get off the ground?*

"Dani, come along, it's almost time to board the plane," Mom said. A tall, lean flight attendant emerged from the side door. We moved forward two-by-two, just like the army soldiers. I froze at the entrance of the aircraft; I couldn't believe what I was seeing. There was an inside staircase right in the middle of the plane and as far as my eyes could see, rows and rows of seats.

I asked the flight attendant "What's up there?"

"It's the upper deck for first class," she replied.

"Keep moving, Daniela," I heard my mother say.

I called shotgun for the window seat. I eagerly stowed my belongings and sat down for the long journey. The force of takeoff thrust my tiny body further back into the seat. I struggled against gravity to get full usage of my window view. The airport and the surrounding buildings and cars became smaller and smaller. Gradually streams of soft, white, cotton-candy clouds passed by until we were fully engulfed and floating amongst them. The captain came on and made announcements about the logistics of the flight. I listened intently as he explained the cruising altitude, the length of the flight and our estimated arrival time in Hawai'i.

Moments later, the in-flight manager made an announcement asking the passengers seated next to the window to lower their shades, because the in-flight movie was about to start. I took another long gander out the window before I closed it.

The flight was silent except for the humming of the engine; most of the passengers were sleeping. I opened my window to pure darkness; I couldn't even see the stars. I enjoyed the peaceful feeling I was experiencing. I too fell asleep and enjoyed the smooth ride of the Braniff International 747 jetliner. My passage to a new life had begun.

Bug-eyed, I soaked in the spectacular scenery of Hawai'i. I never imagined a place could possess such beauty. All my senses were captured in a blissful euphoria. I twisted and turned the entire drive to Schofield Barracks, our new home. Nestled between two picturesque mountains with luxuriant vegetation thriving all around was where my new home was located. *Yes, the view of my life had changed!* I thought. I pinched myself to ensure I wasn't dreaming. I was stretched across my bed like a snow angel when my mom and Mr. Morehouse peeked into my room.

"How do you like your room?" they asked.

"I love it and I can't wait to decorate it!" I replied

"Just remember no holes in the walls," Mr. Morehouse said.

"Ok, I will just use tape to hang my posters of Prince and Michael Jackson," I said.

"Uncle Sam approves," Mr. Morehouse said.

"Dinner will be ready in 15 minutes," they said as they left my room.

"Ok," I replied. I made a mental note to inquire about this Uncle Sam person.

Laughter and joy filled the atmosphere. Not since Papa's had I seen my family so happy. My siblings were relaxed and cheerful. My mother had a peaceful glow, and although I didn't know much about Mr. Morehouse, even he seemed happy. Dinner had been festive and filled with lively, silly conversation. I didn't want this moment to end. Mom and Richard (We couldn't keep calling him Mr. Morehouse) gave us our respective chores and household duties. To our surprise we would receive an allowance. Stunned, we just sat there emotionless.

"All right guys, you're excused from the table," Richard said.

"Yes, sir," we replied.

The first six months went by quickly, and to my surprise, so did my adjustment to living in Hawai'i. I had made new friends and was thriving in school. However, confusion and conflict invaded my peace of mind. I had grown to care for Richard. He was kind and loving. He opened my mind to different possibilities for my future. At the same time, he was unconsciously teaching me how men should treat me. Richard implemented new structures and rules into our lives. His rules stripped away my self-imposed authority of a surrogate mother to my siblings.

I should have been elated to be freed of such responsibilities, but instead I felt lost, unwanted, and no longer needed. Suddenly, I was off balance and not sure of my place in their lives. I believed I was abandoning them. Anger, happiness, freedom, and responsibility ruled my thoughts. Just to be a child had become foreign, a distant memory. I thought, *what if he leaves us? Who would be here to pick up the pieces? No, I can't rely on him!*

My stepdad did as he usually did, walked in and greeted us, then checked to see if we had completed our chores. "Dani, isn't it your day to wash the dishes?" he asked. I ignored him. He asked again. I reluctantly got off the sofa. I headed towards my bedroom. "Turn around, young lady!" he demanded.

A deep burning sensation started to rise within me. I reached for a knife and started verbally insulting him and taking a stance of a warrior preparing for combat. I am not sure what my stepfather witnessed in me, but somehow in his loving way he was able to console and ease some of the pain that lay in my heart. He gently removed the knife from my hand and lovingly embraced me. In that moment, I had permission to step back into my rightful place as a child. The burden of functioning as an adult had been removed. Love filled my being.

I was so frightened by the experience, I abruptly pulled away and took off running down a long winding trail. The path was lined with the lush vegetation of the Hawai'ian Islands. I ran amongst the hapu'u ferns, banyan, and coconut trees. The sweet fragrance of the hibiscus flowers mesmerized my senses. An eruption was boiling from the deepest part of my core. Explosive tears flowed from my eyes, hitting the pavement violently. I released the darkness within me and gave way to the gentle, healing, rhythmic flow of nature.

When the pain had been expelled, an incredible sense of peace came upon me. It was authentic and sacred. I never had an experience like this before. I knew I was experiencing what I had been searching for since I was a young girl. I had connected with God!

In that moment I was aware I was loved. I stopped running and became very still and rejoiced in the moment. As my thoughts started to invade my consciousness, I reminisced on the many different churches and religious faiths that I had studied. I chuckled to myself that I had found what I had longed for on a winding road in Hawai'i.

Hawai'i was everything that I hoped it to be and more. Being released from adult responsibilities opened the door for me to reconnect with who I was. I started to spread my wings and explore. I made new friends at school and even joined some of the social clubs. I was just beginning to flourish, to find my niche, when I noticed something was trying to clip my wings.

On the surface we all seem to have adjusted to our new life, except for Mom. As our family's happiness expanded, our mother's diminished. She took most of her frustration out on me. Our already-strained relationship began to rapidly deteriorate. The dysfunction that once bonded our union and held us together as a family no longer existed. The dynamics were being reversed and I had been given liberty and freedom to just be a child. She was trying to pull me back to the shackles of my past existence as the family caregiver. I refused to be pulled back into her abyss of discontent and self-pity. I knew I couldn't go back. I had tasted freedom.

Teen night at the skating rink was coming up in a few weeks. Every teen on the base was going. It was going to be the first time the authorities were allowing the rink to stay open until midnight. All my friends were going. Reka, Cynthia and Dotie. We spent countless hours on the phone planning every of detail of our grand entrance. There was only one problem. I hadn't asked for permission to go. I first thought to ask Richard, but I knew he would consult with my mom before giving me an answer.

So I decided to cut the middleman out and deal directly with her. I had been on my best behavior for weeks. Watching my attitude— something she was always complaining about— and forgoing other teen events. It was two days before the party and my friends were getting impatient and demanded that I ask! Ugh, peer pressure! I passed by my parents' bedroom door, and taking a quick peek inside, I saw my mom relaxing across their bed. I took a deep breath and knocked on the door.

"Mom, can I come in?" I said.

"Yes, come in Dani, what's on your mind?"

I started to ramble from one unrelated subject to the next and when I thought I had her fully distracted, I dropped the question. "And so, Mom, can I go the skating rink Friday?" I took one step back and held my breath.

"Dani, you have been talking a mile a minute! Now back up and tell me about the skating party," she said.

"Yes ma'am," I said, then gave her all the details.

"You can go but you must be home by 10:00 PM." I was happy and furious at the same time. I could go but I couldn't stay out as late as I wanted to. I repeated the details again and noted it was the first time the military base was keeping the skating rink open for "teens only" until 12 midnight. That didn't change my mother's decision, so I threw in my trump card and said Reka is going.

My mom was very fond of Reka. Although she thought she was homely looking, she felt Reka had a good head on her shoulders. "10 PM, Dani, now turn out the light," she demanded.

"Good night," I mumbled. I didn't have the courage to call my friends. I just threw my defeated body across the bed and cried myself to sleep.

Cynthia was waiting outside the skating rink when we arrived. "Hey, Cynthia!" we said in unison.

"What took you guys so long?"

"Girl, you know Dani takes forever to get ready," Reka replied. They all laughed. "Where is Dotie?" Dani asked.

"Girl, you know she is probably already in her skates and rolling." We skated and skated; we never wanted to leave the floor. We even came in second place in the skate-off contest. It was the best night of my life!

"Hey party people, we are going to take a quick 15-minute break. We will be back at 10:30 PM," the DJ said. *Did he just say its 10:30PM? No, that can't be right.* My heart was racing. I thought, *I have to get out of here*! I raced to the rental counter to return my skates, when out of the blue I heard someone scream my name.

"Daniela Grace Baldwin!"

I turned in the direction of the voice and found my mother standing in the middle of the rink, screaming at the top of her lungs. I wanted to die.

Reka ran to her friends and asked "Dani, what is your mother doing here?"

I was too embarrassed to answer. My eyes pleaded with Reka to help me.

"Follow me, there is an exit in the back," she said. We four walked in silence all the way home.

My mother's car was parked in the driveway when we arrived at my home. "Reka, I am going to be the laughingstock at school. How could she?"

"Do you want me to come in with you?"

"No. I am pretty sure I will be grounded for life." They laughed. They didn't believe me. But they didn't know my mother.

"How could you disobey me, Dani? You were given a curfew and I expected you to follow it!" I decided silence was my best defense. "So, you have nothing to say?"

"No, ma'am."

"You're grounded. Come straight home when you get out of school."

"Yes ma'am."

After the skating rink fiasco, I consciously decided never to ask her permission to do anything. I would ask Richard for permission for activities I knew she wouldn't object to. For everything else, I would sneak out. I usually was able to sneak in and out without her noticing, but tonight, I had barely unlatched my window, when my mother busted through my door. She lunged forward and swung a broomstick at me!

She cried out, "You are my stupid mistake! I gave up my dreams because of you!"

I grabbed the stick midair and screamed, "No, I am not your mistake!"

Our eyes met and spoke the words neither of us could verbally express. I wished she could have spoken what her eyes revealed. I longed to hear those precious words that every daughter wants to hear from her mother. Instead, she just turned and walked away, leaving me to question my value to her. I whispered, "Please come back," as she slammed the door. I fell to my knees, hoping she would return and cradle me in the security of her bosom, while knowing she never would. My feelings of loneliness and sadness enveloped me.

I ran away to a family friend's home. I stayed away from home for three days before my mother insisted that I return. Deep inside I was happy to return home. I had quickly discovered that running away wasn't as glamorous as I thought it would be. I was excited when I saw my stepdad turning into my friend's driveway.

"Dani, are you ok? Did anyone hurt you?" Richard asked. I was stunned, he seemed sincere. "Dani, we all missed you."

Yeah, everyone but Mom, I thought. "I am ok, and no one hurt me," I finally replied.

I wanted to say so many things to my stepdad. I wanted to tell him that I loved him and that I was sorry for all the trouble I had been. But I didn't have the courage to expose my heart. Disappointed in myself, I just stared out the window all the way home.

My stepdad's tour of duty in Hawai'i was ending and soon we would be uprooted to another military base. I had mixed emotions about this. I was very sad we were leaving. I had grown to love my life in Hawai'i. I was voted Princess of the Island of Kaua'i in the Wahiawa Middle School pageant. And I had had my first experience with love.

Although Richard said it was just puppy love, I truly believed I was in love. because I felt blissfully foolish and scared to death at the same time. I remembered one weekend I was so adamant about seeing him, I talked my best friend into coming along with me to spy on him. And when the short-term relationship was over, I felt all the heartache and pain associated with love. I remember sitting in front of the stereo playing the song "Always and Forever" over and over again.

At the same time I was excited about going back to the mainland and being somewhat closer to my family, I was equally as frightened about going to a new high school and the daunting task of fitting in and making new friends. To celebrate our departure, my father planned a family BBQ at the beach. To make the occasion even more special, my favorite grandmother Eva was visiting that week. Everyone was excited, but no one more so than me. I ran to the window every time I heard a car pull into our complex. The stress of waiting for her arrival was killing me.

I had a hundred questions to ask her. It is through her stories I learned about our family history. "She's here!" my older brother yelled. We raced to the door trying to be the first to hug her.

"Hello Grandma," I eagerly said.

"Hello baby," she replied. I selfishly wanted to whisk her away and have her all to myself.

"Dani, you guys take Eva's things to the guest room."

"Ok," I said. We spent the rest of the evening catching up on the happenings on the mainland.

"All right everyone, we're leaving for camp at the break of dawn," Richard said. "Let's get some rest, morning will be here before you know it!"

When we arrived at the beach, we were all anxious to get to the water. "Before you kids take off running, help unload the car first," my mother said. She seemed agitated today. I thought, *I'll keep clear of her*. I practically unloaded the car by myself, trying to avoid any confrontation. It seemed the more I tried to help her and be the daughter she wanted me to be, the angrier she became. She lashed out at me every moment she could. I wanted to lash back out at her. I wanted to ask her why she hates me! She was killing my self-esteem so much! I ran back to the car to get the rest of the things we had packed, just to get away from her.

Moments later my angel appeared. "Why does she hate me so much?" I asked my grandma. I didn't really expect an answer, but my grandma's eyes said everything.

She simply replied, "It's not just you; she is angry with me too." I was relieved, because at least I was right in my thoughts, and someone had validated my feelings.

"Grandma, why does she treat me so badly? Do you know she even told me that she loves me but doesn't like me? What kind of a mother says that to her child? I am not her mistake," I sobbed. "Grandma you better go before she comes over here. I will be ok."

"Go wash your face Baby and come and eat."

"Okay." I did go and wash up but decided to take a long walk on the beach instead of being near my mother. I sat down to watch the waves as they crashed against the shoreline. I longed to have my father in my life. I imagined he would love and protect me always. I laughed at the silliness of my daydream. My father wanted no part of me either. I remembered the last time I waited for him. *It was a colorful, cool autumn day. I sat on the cold concrete steps waiting for my father. I could see my Grandma*

Eva peeking through the curtains to check on me. Deep inside I had high
hopes of spending time with my father. I prayed he would show up this
time and not punish me for refusing his love years ago. As the hours
passed by, the temperature rose, and my hope diminished.

"*Dani, come on in now. You can wait for your father inside,*" Grandma
Eva said.

"*I'll be right in.*" After a few moments, I gave up. I could no
longer avoid the shame of being deserted again.

A voice interrupted my memories. "Dani, your mother
has been calling you. The food is ready, and we are all waiting
for you."

"I am sorry Richard; I didn't hear her. I was just sitting
here thinking."

"I don't know about you, but I am starving. I could eat a
horse." We both started laughing. To keep the peace, I avoided
my mother for the rest of the day.

The years passed and we moved from base to base as my
stepfather moved forward in his military career. But one day it was
time for me to move away from the family and start my own life.

My stepfather's last tour of duty was in Germany. He was
stationed on the military base of Hanau, which is approximately
40 minutes from Frankfurt, depending on how fast you drove
on the *autobahn.* Living in Europe was magical; all the countries
I wanted to see were just hours away by car and I took full
advantage of every opportunity. I absolutely never wanted to leave.

When my stepdad announced that his time was up in Germany, I was devastated. I knew I had to stay; it was the one place I fit. I pleaded my case to my stepdad first. One evening, I found him in his study reading. I thought, *it's now or never.*

"Richard, do you have a moment?" I asked as I entered. I didn't want to give him an out.

"Yes, sure Dani, come on in."

"I don't want to leave Germany. I love it here! I am in school and have a great job. Well, the job is not the best but it's a government job and it pays well." When he didn't interrupt me, I continued. "My friend Ming said I could share an apartment with her. What do you think, can I stay?" I let out a sigh of relief at getting all this out.

"Dani, I actually think it's a great idea, but it's not me you must convince. I can see you're thriving, and you have a sensible head on your shoulders and technically you are an adult."

"I know, that's why I am coming to you first, maybe you can help me convince her? Can you talk with her today?"

"Yes, I will speak with her today."

"Thank you!"

I was a ball of nerves today at work. I couldn't help but run different scenarios of what my mom's reaction would be when Richard shared with her my desires.

The next day, I waited until we were alone to approach her about my remaining in Germany. Although her bedroom door was open, to announce my presence I lightly tapped on it. "Mom, do you have a moment to talk?"

"Yes, come in."

"Did Richard talk to you about my plans to stay here in Germany?"

"Yes, and the answer is no. Although you may think you're grown, you're not!"

"I am eighteen, soon to be nineteen, and I have been taking care of myself for a long time. I buy all my clothing and food. I am paying for college, and I have a good job making really good money. How is that not taking care of myself?"

"You're just not ready and that's my decision."

This time I couldn't let it go, I had to fully speak my mind. "Mom, that doesn't make any sense, I took care of my siblings when we moved out of Papa's house. In fact I practically raised my younger brother. Honestly, I have been on my own taking care of me for quite some time, even as I lived under your roof! You can't stop me!"

"We will see!"

I stormed out of the room, grabbed my books, and headed off to class. I wanted to believe she would have a change of heart but deep inside I knew she had made her decision and would do everything possible to keep me from living in Germany.

Returning to the red dirt of Oklahoma brought back memories I thought I had buried. I couldn't breathe there. It became my sole mission to escape. I put my plan into action. I enrolled in college and started working, but I grew impatient; my thoughts were on exotic and mysterious destinations. I was drowning there and no one seemed to notice or care.

One day while channel surfing, I ran across a nature show. There was a beautiful monarch butterfly on the screen. Immediately I heard the words "Wondering Butterfly" and I foolishly turned around in hopes of seeing my Great-Grandmother Maikoda standing by. I thought, *I know my Great Grandmother Maikoda is trying to tell me something, but what? What would she say if she was here?*

She would tell me that all the answers I seek are within me. I sat for hours thinking of my desires and pondering my options. I knew my current plan would not work for me. I needed out, now! I pulled out my journal and started writing down what I most desired and prayed for guidance. I still wanted to see the world, and I decided a career in the airline industry could give me the chance to fulfill my dreams.

I graduated from the Northwest School of Airline Travel in November and was employed by December. The job was located far away from the red dirt state of Oklahoma! I now resided in Los Angeles. The years flew by as I lived my life on my terms. I blinked and 20 years had passed…

"Good morning, how are you?"

I looked at the bus driver and rolled my eyes as I continued to my seat. The next day, as soon as the bus doors opened, I heard "Good morning!" I thought, *crap not this guy again.* I ignored him again. Every time I looked up, I found him staring at me through his rear-view mirror.

The next few days, I parked in the airport parking lot just to avoid the bus driver. However, I knew I couldn't keep paying the high fees, not on my salary. I decided to arrive to work earlier than usual, and it worked at first, but hanging out with my colleagues in the wee hours of the morning was taking its toll. At times I was only getting two hours of sleep. This was too much work just to avoid this guy.

"Hello and before you ignore me, I would like to introduce myself. My name is Mark Okafor and I just think you're beautiful." I didn't care what he thought. I just wanted the guy to leave me alone.

"Ok, great. Now leave me alone." I couldn't believe I what had just came out of mouth. I thought, *what else could I have done, the guy just* didn't *get it, I wasn't interested.* After, this incident, I didn't see Mark driving any of the buses I took. I would see him around work, but he never approached me.

"Dani, you're needed out front to sign for a package."

"Tina, can you sign it for me; I am terrible busy."

"Dani, I tried but he says it must be signed by the recipient." Reluctantly, I got up from my chair to see. What could be so important that it had to be signed by me? I gasped for air when I turned the corner; a dozen long-stemmed red roses, with pink carnations and a hint of baby breath, enticed my senses. Tina reached for the card,

"Here you go," she said.

Playfully, I snatched the card out of her hand and started to walk away.

"Come back here and read the card," she said. The other employees crowded around. I knew we wouldn't get any work done until I read the card.

"Okay, I'll read the damn card. It says, *Hello Beautiful, I hope you're having a good day.*

"Now get back to work." I turned to walk away.

"Excuse me," Tina said as she cleared her throat. I knew they wanted to know who the flowers were from, but honestly, I didn't know either, as he had failed to sign it.

"I never kiss and tell," I said, and walked away. Moments later, there was a knock at the door. I thought, *it could be only one person.*

"Come in Tina."

"Well, who is the guy?"

"I don't know, but I have a strong suspicion it's the guy from the bus," I replied. I continued to receive gifts from my secret admirer for about a week.

"Hello, Dani," he said with a heavy accent. When I looked up from my desk, there he was, the culprit. I don't know how I knew it would be him, but I did.

"Hi, it's you who has been sending me the flowers and gifts?"

"Yes, did you enjoy them?"

"The gifts were nice, but please don't send anymore. In fact, I'll return the others."

"No, please keep them, I cannot accept them back."

"Look, your name is Mark?" He nodded. "Mark, I really appreciate the effort but you're not my type and I really want you to respect my wishes."

"How do you know I am not your type?"

I thought, *good comeback.* "Because you're not. Now I need to get back to work." I felt awkward. I didn't know how to end this conversation and it didn't seem like he was going to move at all. The phone rang, giving me my out. "I need to get that, goodbye."

Mark began showing up at all the places I liked to hang out. How he knew where I would be bothered me. I ignored him as best I could, but he was relentless in his pursuit. After a week of his intrusion, I decided to get the 411 on him and I knew exactly who to ask. Caryn Miles. She knew everything about everyone at the job.

"Caryn, what's the scoop on the new bus driver?" She looked confused, so I began to describe him.

"Oh, that's Mark Okafor. He just transferred from Canada, I think? Why, girl, do you like him?" she asked.

I had to be careful with my response. I could hear her wheels turning. "No, it's nothing like that, I was checking for someone else," I said.

"Sure," she said.

"Thanks girl," I said as I quickly walked away. I thought *bad decision to involve her in my business.*

"Thank god it's Friday," my friend said as we exited the employee bus.

"Hey Dani, do you have any plans?"

"No, not at the moment."

"Me either. I thought I would just play it by ear."

"Sounds like a plan, call me later if you decide to do something."

"Sure, see ya later." In the distance, I could see a guy standing near my car. Initially I didn't pay attention, because often times after work people would stand around just talking. But as I got closer, I could see it was that bus driver guy. I looked around to see if anyone else was in the lot. There was no one nearby. I thought, *this guy is annoying.*

"What are you doing and why are you near my car?"

"You will either get into my car or I will get into yours. I am going to take you out to dinner," he said.

I had never been given an ultimatum before, but here I was staring down the barrel of one. I thought, *what is this, some type of primitive caveman shit?*

Frustrated, I said, "I'll follow you to the restaurant, but I am not getting into your car."

During dinner he talked for what seemed like an eternity about nothing that interested me. I faded in and out of the conversation, only chiming in when necessary. I was perplexed; I did not know how to get rid of this guy. I had come to the conclusion that being uncivil was not the answer. At our last encounter, I was extremely rude and yet here we were having dinner. *Why had I agreed to do this? Was it because I was used to obeying my mother, even when I didn't like what she was forcing me to do?*

I thought, *what was I going to do? I know, I'll try letting him down easy.* Looking him square in the eyes I said, "Mark, I don't like you. I think you're a nice guy, but I am not interested." I didn't wait for a response because I wanted to leave with a dramatic effect, hoping it would further drive my conviction home, so I forcefully grabbed my purse and stormed out of the restaurant. I was both pleased with my decision and excited that I had made such an exit. I hoped this would be the end of his following me. Hopefully, I had finally gotten through his head that I *was not interested!*

To my surprise, two weeks later he was back on the prowl and with reinforcements. He was attacking his prey from all fronts by soliciting a mutual acquaintance to aid him in his conquest. My friends believed I had misjudged him and thought I should at least give him another opportunity.

"Hey, I have a great idea. Why don't we all go out together?" Eddie said.

"I am in," Candye said.

I looked over at Leandro and Claudia. I thought, *why did I even look over at them? I wasn't in the mood to go out.* But old programming of being agreeable even when I wanted to say "No" kicked in. Despite my desire to the contrary, I succumbed to peer pressure.

"How about tonight?" Eddie said.

"Tonight?"

"Girl, don't act like you have plans." They all started laughing.

"Ok, where are we going? I'll meet you guys there."

"Oh, you got jokes. I know you Dani, and you'll find some excuse not to come. So, we are picking you up, be ready at 8:00pm."

"Eddie, you get on my nerves!"

"I know, that's why you love me." Eddie was right, I did love him. He was the first person I met when I moved to Los Angeles and had become one of my closest friends.

"Dani, dress casual, no heels."

"Ok."

I could hear the music as they drove into my driveway. I grabbed my keys and ran out the door. I stopped dead in my tracks when Mark got out of the car.

"Hello, I was coming to your door," Mark said.

"It's not that, I just…" Before, I could complete my sentence Eddie added his two cents.

"Dani, stop acting shocked, you had to know he was riding with us."

"Shut up Eddie!" I thought, *this is going to be a long night.*

"Hello, Candye."

"Hey girl, you are looking good."

"Where are Leandro and Claudia?"

"They are meeting us there." I was trying to avoid Mark as long as possible.

"Where is there?"

"You'll find out soon."

"Mark, do you know where we are going?"

"No, I actually don't. They said it is one of your favorite places."

"Alrighty, then."

"Dani, I would like to start over with you if that's possible." I thought, *what is he talking about? There was never a start.*

"Let me explain. I realize for you I may have come on too strong and I apologize for my aggressive behavior."

I wasn't sure what he was trying to say. But at least he had apologized.

"Hi, my name Mark."

I thought, *what the hell is he doing?* Then he extended his hand.

"Oh, my name is Dani." I felt silly but played along. "Where is your accent from?"

"What accent?" I looked at him like, *really?*

He smiled. "I am from Nigeria."

"Uh, ok."

For what seemed like an hour, he talked about his country. I started to get restless. "Eddie, how much longer until we get there?"

"We are almost there."

Oh my, we were going to Magic Mountain. They were right, · I loved amusement parks. The weather was perfect, and the parks are always open later in the summer. We all had a blast, riding roller coasters, playing games and eating. All in all, it was a fun evening.

Mark was respectful when he walked me to my door. "Dani, when can I see you again?"

"I don't know."

"Dani, just give me a chance," he asked.

"Mark, I have to be honest. I know you like me, but I don't have the same feelings for you."

"I am up for the challenge."

"As long as we are on the same page."

"That's fair, can I get your phone number?"

"Sure."

After giving him my number, I rushed inside, just in case he got any ideas about kissing me.

We began dating and traveling around the country extensively. Our favorite weekend destination was Las Vegas. We practically drove down every weekend from Los Angeles. "So, what would you say if I asked you to marry me?" he asked.

Without hesitation, I said "No." I was starting to feel comfortable with him, but my core feelings had not changed.

"Mark, I don't want to have this conversation again, please. You are a great guy, but I am not in love with you."

"Dani, I have enough love for both of us. I love you and want to spend the rest of my life with you."

"I am sorry Mark, but I just don't feel the same way. We have only been dating a few months."

"It's been five-and-a-half months."

"Mark, you're going way too fast. I just agreed to let you move in with me and honestly, I am not really comfortable with that decision." In a moment of weakness I had agreed to let him move in with me, but I was still unsure of why I had done this.

"I know you're not, but you will see everything will work out fine.'

I thought, *I hope so, I can't bail out now, he has already given his notice to his landlord.*

He pulled a small box out of his pocket and handed it to me. "Would you please wear this ring while you think about it?" I didn't want to wear his ring, but I reluctantly slipped it onto my finger.

"I'll bring some of my things over tomorrow after work. Good night."

I was glad it was my day off as I barely slept a wink. I just couldn't get comfortable last night. I was sure it was just my nerves; I had never lived with a guy. Had I made a bad decision? I looked at the ring on my finger. I picked up my to-do list, but quickly set it back down. I was too on edge to think about running errands. I thought, *it's just going to be a lazy day*. Just as I started toward my bedroom, the phone rang. I looked at the clock; it was 9:00 AM.

"Hello."

"Um, is this Daniela?" It was a woman's voice. I thought, *nobody calls me Daniela, not any of my friends. It must be sales call or something.*

"Who is asking?"

"You drive a red Toyota, right?"

What kind of creepy question was this? My nerves, already on edge, stretched tighter.

"Are you asking me or confirming it? Who is this?"

I could hear children in the background. Oddly enough, I was curious about this lady. "Hello, lady what can I help you with?"

"You are sleeping with my husband."

I almost dropped the phone in shock. "What the hell are you talking about? You have the wrong person!"

"My husband's name is Mark Okafor." My heart stopped. I sat down, feeling lightheaded.

"I didn't think you knew. I mean, you are a lot younger than him. I found your marriage application."

"What? Marriage application? What are you talking about? Marriage application? I think you have the wrong person. I am not getting married."

"Were you in Las Vegas two weeks ago?"

This was getting weirder. My heart was in my throat. How did she know this?

"Yes, but we go to Vegas almost every weekend."

"I know." Right at that moment, I knew she was telling the truth. My heart fell.

"Oh my god, I am so sorry, I didn't know, please believe me I didn't know. You will never have to worry about me again. I am so very sorry." I hung up the phone and fury took over! My first thought was to go to Mark's job and confront him. I thought, *I can't go there acting like a maniac; after all I worked there too.*

I called every number at the airport until I located him. "Mark, we need to talk right now."

"Can it wait until I get off?"

At the top of my lungs, I screamed, "You either come here right now or I am coming there and bringing your wedding ring!" I hung up the phone. I felt so deceived, how could I not know, why didn't I know? How could he have kept something like this from me for almost six months? How could he ask me to marry him while he had a family and a wife already?

I was sitting on the couch when he arrived. I had so many questions and so much anger, I wanted to jump up and scratch his eyes out! "Why, Mark?" were the only words I could articulate.

"Dani, let me explain. I never meant to hurt…"

I interrupted him; I didn't want to hear those words. "Huh, you didn't want to hurt me! What about *your wife*? How could you put me in this situation? Can you imagine how I felt when your *wife* called?"

"I understand."

"You understand? You don't understand *shit!* You know what, get out!"

"Dani, please give me a moment. You have two minutes?" He dropped to his knees. "You see, I don't love her. I was planning to get a divorce."

"*Planning* to get a divorce? Get out and don't ever come back!"

"Dani   "

"I said get out! Go home to your *wife!*"

The next few weeks, I questioned myself over and over again. *How did I miss the signs? What are the signs?* I never saw a ring on his finger, but I didn't even remember looking for one. I thought about all the time we spent together. The trips to Vegas every weekend. What was he telling her? The other detail she shared about him being older than me concerned me. I knew he was older, but how much? The way she said it, it sounded like a considerable age difference between us. Was this just another lie he has told me? I thought, *what a way to end the year. A May-December romance with a bigamist. Well, at least it ended before we got married. I was through with him, and glad to be on my own again.*

New Year's Eve I was excited as my friends and I were preparing to ring in the New Year. I was the fifth wheel, but I didn't mind because they were my support team. At the stroke of midnight, we danced and screamed to the top of our lungs!

"Dani, what did you wish for?" Eddie asked.

"You know Eddie, I really didn't ask for anything specific, just to be happy."

"I used my wish for you Dani."

"Oh, that is so sweet of you Eddie."

"I hope you find someone special."

"Ah, thank you but…"

"That's my wish, end of story!" We laughed and hugged each other.

We finished our night hanging out at the beach. Everyone split up and headed in different directions. Standing alone I looked up to the heavens and wondered if love was for me or if I was destined to be alone.

The new year started quickly. One day I wanted to hide my head in the sand like an ostrich, and the next day it was Valentine's Day. I picked up an extra shift to avoid all of the love birds. The flight loads were always extremely light on holiday evenings, so I brought a book to pass the time. After 6:00 PM the airport terminal was practically empty. I went to my favorite area and watched as the planes took off. I looked up from my book and was startled by Mark standing in front of me.

"Hi Dani, how are you?"

"What are you doing here?"

"I just saw you sitting here and thought I would come over and say hello."

"Well, you have said hello. Now leave."

"Ok, but just so you know, I divorced my wife."

"And?"

"Well, I just wanted you to know." I picked up my book and started to read again. I thought, *I can't open my heart to him or anyone else. Been there, done that. It just hurts too much.*

By the end of February, I started working a second job to help make ends meet. I was still living in the apartment that Mark and I were supposed to share together. Although it was a little over my budget, I loved the location; everything was within walking distance.

From time to time, Mark would wander into my work area, but he wouldn't stay long. But today he lingered until the flight departed and everyone left the gate area.

"What do you want?"

"Dani, you never gave a chance to explain…"

"You don't get it, there is nothing to explain. You are married."

"I was married, I am not any longer."

"So, congratulations. Do you want a cookie?"

"No, but I would love to take you out to dinner tonight."

My immediate thought was *Hell no*, but honestly, I wanted to know why he betrayed me. "Why?"

"Dani, I just want a chance to explain."

"Ok, I'll meet you. Where are we going?"

"Is Mexican ok?"

"Sure."

"How about Guadalupe's at 8:00 PM."

Fridays at Guadalupe's were always festive. The mariachi band was always fun to watch and sometimes my friends and I would dance. I started the conversation. "Mark, so what happened that day after you left my apartment?"

"I went home, and my wife and I talked. I told her that it was over between us, and it had been for a while. I moved her back to Kansas and we finalized our divorce."

"Do you guys have kids together?"

"Yes, a girl." Mark gave me his version of what went wrong with the marriage. I sat and listened, but it still didn't change the fact that he had lied to me.

"Dani, I don't want this night to end. Do you want to drive to the beach?"

I paused for a few moments before answering. I thought, *hell no!* on one hand, but on the other I was lonely, I hadn't dated since we broke up. *It's not like we are getting back together*, I justified it to myself. *It's just a walk on the beach.*

"Ok, the drive will be nice."

We went by my apartment to drop off my car. I ran up to quickly change and Mark followed. We never saw the beach that evening. Secretly, I started spending time with him. I didn't want my friends to know I was back with Mark after what he had done to me. I reasoned with myself that it was just for a little while.

By March we were living together. It didn't take him long to start pushing for us to get married. I ignored him as long as I could until one day, I couldn't take it.

"Mark, my feelings for you haven't changed. I am sorry to say, but I don't love or trust you. I mean there is still so much I don't know about you."

"Dani, there is nothing else to know. I have shared everything with you."

"I don't believe you. Whatever happened to your first wife in Canada? Or was she your first wife?"

"Dani, look, I am here with you. That's all that matters."

I thought, *I am tired of trying to get the truth.* "Mark, you're always talking about how secretive I am, but it looks like you're the one with the secrets. So, when you come clean with your secrets, I'll think about trusting you!"

I grabbed my car keys and left. Not knowing where to go, I just sat in my car thinking. *I know he is hiding something; I just know it. Otherwise, why is he so desperate to get married?*

"Dani, I am glad you're back. Come and sit next to me."

"Mark, I am tired. I am going to bed."

"Just give me a few moments." I sat down in the chair.

"Remember when I told you that my family was attacked in Nigeria, and we had to flee to save our lives?"

"Yes, you already told me about your family being attacked by some regime and how they struck you in the back of your head with a machete."

"I, well, I ended up in Canada where I married my first wife. It was hard for me to find work, so I came to America to find work. My wife didn't want to come to the US, so eventually we divorced."

"So, you stayed and married another woman and failed to tell me. What I want to know is, are you legal to be here?"

"Yes, I have a work permit."

"Is that all it takes to stay here in the US?"

"Yes, for now."

"I don't understand any of this. What does *for now* mean?"

"It means I am legal to work in America."

"Ok, if you say so. One last thing, your wife said something about a green card and that you needed me to get one."

"She is just bitter."

"Well, I am going to bed."

"Good night, Dani."

Mark backed off about getting married for a few weeks and things seemed to be back to normal. Then one evening he pulled out a photo of his mother and sister in Lagos and he started reminiscing about happier times in his country.

"You know, Dani, I just miss them so much."

"Then why don't you go and visit them?"

"That's part of the problem; we got separated after the attack. It will take me a while to find them. Besides if I leave, they may not let me back in." Dani didn't respond. "Dani, please believe me. I don't need you for a green card because I am legal to work here. But my work permit does not allow me to leave the country."

"So, what are you saying exactly?" Mark knew he was wearing her down.

"I am saying I want to find my family. I want them to meet you. Dani, will you marry me?"

"Mark, we have just been together again since March and I am not ready now, or maybe never. Besides, I simply don't trust you."

I felt sorry for him and his family, but I was still against marrying him.

My bawling was so noticeable that the preacher stopped the ceremony. He asked his assistant to help me compose myself. "Are you ok?" he asked.

Before I could gather my words, Mark intervened. "She is just a little nervous," he said. "Yeah, and the July heat is not helping matters," he continued.

The preacher lifted his left brow suspiciously, looked me dead in the eye, and said "Little lady, are you ok? Do you want me to continue?"

I nodded yes, out of an obligation to save face. The preacher continued with the nuptials. During the vows I thought *why didn't I have the courage to stand up for myself? How could I be so weak in this area of my life? I am crying out of some deep shame and sadness and don't have a clue to what it is.* I felt the pressure of Mark's hand and realized they were waiting for my reply to seal the contract. After the ceremony was over, driving down the Vegas strip felt surreal.

"Mark, can we just go and cancel it?" I sadly asked.

"Don't be silly. Dani, I promise to make you happy," he said.

"Dani, we have been married for six months and we have yet to tell your family. Are you ashamed of me or something?" I thought, *how do you explain to your family that you married someone you don't love? I can't, because I can't even explain it to myself!*

"I promise I will, soon."

"That's what you always say. I think we should tell them together and guess what, I think right now would be perfect."

"I'm not doing this today and when I do decide, I will tell them by myself!"

"So, how will you explain me when your mother comes next week?"

"Explain what? She knows we live together. Stop overreacting."

"Dani, what will she say when she sees the ring? By the way, where is your ring?"

"I don't know, it's somewhere in the room. Mark it's not like a traditional ring, she probably won't even notice it. Look, I promise, I will tell her soon. Now can we go? I'm starving."

All weeklong I contemplated when I would tell my mom that I was married. I thought, *if I tell her too soon, then everyone in the family would be calling me with suspicious thoughts. They would all assume I got married because I was pregnant. I definitely didn't want to wait until she arrived, because Mark would entertain all of her questions and somehow make it about him.*

"Dani, I just been cleared a seat on the flight, I'll see you soon," my mom said.

"Great, I will be in the gate lobby area when you arrive. Oh, by the way Mom, Mark and I got married."

"What did you say? I didn't hear you; the flight attendant was talking."

"We got married."

"Oh?" There was a tone in her voice I recognized from when I was a child and argued with her. A chill went down my spine.

"We will talk about it when you arrive."

"Ah, ok." I let out a long sigh. I thought *this is going to be a very intense ride from the airport.* "Mark, I am leaving to pick up my mom."

"Are you sure you don't want me to come?"

Having Mark there was the last thing I wanted. "Yes, see you later."

I asked the gate agent for permission to assist my mother, who was traveling with my six-month-old nephew. After all the passengers deplaned, I went on board.

"Hey Mom, I see your hands are full. Are these your things in the overhead bin? How was your trip? Did the baby sleep all the way?" I was so nervous I just continued to babble about inconsequential matters.

"The flight was fine, and Jason slept the entire way. How are you doing?"

I reached out my hands to take the baby. "Let me hold my nephew."

"Where is Mark?"

"He is at home. I thought we should, I mean we could, have some private time."

As soon as we loaded the bags and fastened Jason in, Lela started right in with her questions. "So how long have you guys been married?"

"For six months."

"Six months! Dani, I can't believe you've been married for six months, and you hit me with the information moments before the flight took off! Well, I know you're not pregnant, not that that would matter. Can you tell me why you chose to keep it a secret from your family?"

"Mom, you know me, I never wanted to get married or have kids. I guess I am still trying to wrap my head around the situation too."

"Well, do you at least love him?"

I hesitated longer than I expected to. For some reason I wasn't ready for that question.

"Uhm, yeah." She gave me a dubious look.

"Why the delay in your answer?"

"Mom, I don't know. I guess I wasn't expecting the question. Enough about me, tell me what's going on at home."

Lela knew she had gotten all that she was going to get out of her daughter. She thought, *I'll drop it for now.*

Mark jumped up when he heard the car pull into the garage. He ran to the passenger side of car to greet my mother. With a smile as big as the moon and arms stretched out as wide as the Earth, he embraced her.

"Hello Mom!" he said. My mom was grinning from ear to ear. I thought, *he has won her over.*

"Hello Mark, it's nice to see you again."

"Here, let me help you get out." The two of them practically walked hand-in- hand into the house. I sat in the car with the baby for a few moments longer. I needed to gather my strength. I walked in to find them chatting and looking rather comfortable on the couch. I walked over and gave the baby to my mother.

"Mark, can you help me get the bags out of the car?"

"Sure, Honey."

Oh lord, Honey? It's starting already. He is going to spread the charm on thickly, and I know my mother will buy into it, and blame me for any problems Mark and I have. Lord, give me strength to make it through this week. "Mark, no matter how much my mom pries, do not tell her anything. I have said all I am going to say about our marriage."

Surprisingly, the week went very well, and I was a little sad to see her go. But what shocked me the most was how much I enjoyed my time with my nephew. After spending the week with him, I was stunned at my capacity to give love and to receive it. I had never wanted children before, but after my time with my nephew, something had definitely shifted inside of me.

From that moment on, all I could think about was having a child. The problem was, I wasn't sure if I could have children. A few years earlier, I had a cyst removed off my ovaries and since we didn't always use protection, I assumed I wasn't able to have children. I decided to put the thought out of my mind, but the longing for a baby persisted.

I started researching ways to improve our chances of conceiving. I started taking extra vitamins and tracking the days that I was ovulating. I even had Mark switch from briefs to boxers. A few months later, we were expecting our first child. Although I was elated that I was pregnant, I was frightened that my baby might be a girl. I just didn't feel like I could love a girl.

"Good morning, Honey, how are you guys doing?"

"We are doing good. I just finished reading to him."

"Dani, why do you keep referring to our baby as a boy? What if it's a girl?"

"I don't know, I just feel like it's a boy. I had better get back to work." I hung up before he could continue. I thought, *what if he is right? What if it's a girl? Will I be able to love her? All I could think about was I wouldn't want my baby girl to suffer like I have.*

I remembered the first time my mother said she loved me. I was twenty years old and had just started my career with an airline. I was in my hotel room on the phone with my mother. She was rambling from one subject to another. I was barely paying attention until she said, "I love you."

I was so shocked by the words I fell off the bed. I thought, *did she say what I thought I heard or was it just my imagination?* Unexpected emotion strangled my vocal chords. Finally, she broke the silence and ended the call. I was relieved because I couldn't reciprocate her words. I was in a state of shock and disbelief. I thought, *how dare she confuse me with an act of love? Where were those words years ago when I longed to hear them?*

"It's a boy!" Mark yelled. "He's got all ten toes and fingers and a head full of hair. His birthmark is located just above his right thigh." Mark was giving me an account of our son's physical appearance and praised the doctors for keeping our son safe, because many babies were being kidnapped right out of the hospital.

I was anxious to see my son. "How much longer?" I asked.

"Here he is." Mark gently handed our newborn son into my arms.

We named our son Jamal. The first time I looked upon his face I was astonished at the miracle that God had entrusted to me. I loved him instantly. When our eyes locked, we each shed a tear.

The first year of Jamal's life was incredible. Each day he did something amazing and we relished each milestone in his life. For the first time in my life, I felt like I had a purpose, a reason for being. I discovered that I had the capacity to give love. As my love for my son grew, my love for myself increased as well.

This new-found self-love made me look at my marriage and how I didn't love Mark. I couldn't keep hiding behind this masquerade of a marriage. I was in a loveless marriage and my heart was filled with anger and contempt towards my husband. Mark was a great dad and doted on Jamal as much as I did. But I feared the long-term effect of raising Jamal in an unhappy home. I thought, *how much longer can I live like this?*

Mark and I were making love, when suddenly, a wicked vision flashed across my mind. I squeezed my eyes tight to erase what I had remembered; but with each thrust of his manhood, the memory became more vivid. I lay still, staring at the ceiling, wanting and waiting for his invasion to be over. When I couldn't stomach anymore, I commanded all my strength and lifted my husband off of me and curled into a fetal position.

I could hear my husband, as from a distance, trying to reach me, but I was trapped in the mirrored vision of a familiar predator stealing my childhood innocence. The visions were flashing in and out like an ambulance light-bar on a high-speed chase; bobbing and weaving through traffic to get its victim to safety. "No, it can't be," I continuously chanted until I fell into a deep sleep.

The sounds of a new day started to creep into my subconscious, and for a brief moment I believed I had dreamt the betrayal of my chastity, until the onslaught of visions invaded my thoughts as I awakened. I felt dirty and jumped into the shower. Sorrowful, I stood in the scorching water, desperately trying to erase the memories of my stolen innocence, but it was futile. The pain was too deep for me to reach. Drained and filled with anguish, I crawled back into bed.

"Hello, Sleeping Beauty, are you feeling better?" he asked. When I didn't answer, he came closer to the bed. I unconsciously jumped. "Dani, are you ok? Do you want to talk about last night?" he asked.

"No," I replied. Sensing my uneasiness, he backed away.

"Would you like a cup of tea?" he asked.

I mumbled "Yes."

I stayed in a comatose state for three days, trying to make sense of my life and the newly exposed memories. I scrutinized every detail and every person in my life, trying to make sense of them. I wondered why this hadn't been spoken about when I was still at home. Why had the rape been hidden? Why had I buried these memories, and what prompted their uncovering now?

I found that I had more questions than answers. Instinctively, I wanted to run far away and sort out my life, but my life had become complicated. I was no longer alone. I had to consider my son and husband.

I decided to share with my husband the visions that were unraveling my life. He listened with compassion and understanding, until I refused to name my predator.

"Who did this to you, Dani?" he asked.

I could barely speak the name to myself; how could I share it with him? I knew I wasn't ready to divulge this information. "The name doesn't matter. I just wanted to share with you what's going on with me emotionally!" I said.

"Why can't you tell me?" he demanded.

"Because I don't want to. I may never want to!" Feeling frustrated, I got up to leave.

"Why are you running off Dani? Stay. We can work this out."

I had wanted to wait until I could think clearly about our marriage, but as usual his persistence pushed me to my breaking point. "I want a divorce!" I yelled. Silence engulfed the room.

"What?"

"Yes, I want out of this shamble of a marriage. I've never lied to you about my feelings. I am suffocating here. Please try to understand," I begged.

"Where is this coming from? What does our marriage have to do with your little episode?"

"Maybe nothing, but then maybe everything! All I know is I need breathing space and time to clear my head and figure me out!"

"I hate when you speak in riddles." These were the last words I heard him say as I slammed the door.

Although the thought of raising a child alone was terrifying, staying in my current situation was more frightening. Mark moved out two days later. It was the first time in a long time that I could take a deep breath and feel a sense of space.

No sooner had I taken that breath, my world began to crumble. Within a week Mark had obtained an attorney and filed for a divorce. I was fine with him wanting a divorce; after all, I had never lied to him about my feelings. But as I further examined the petition, I saw he was also fighting for full custody of Jamal.

I couldn't believe what I was seeing, not from the man who had confessed his undying love a multitude of times. I thought, *my income will not support an attorney, this apartment and childcare. I have got to try to reason with him.* We scheduled a time to meet.

I couldn't sleep. My mind was so active, I kept repeating to myself how I hoped our impending conversation would go. I would promise him that I would never keep Jamal from him. I would remind him of our shared interests and the values we hoped to instill upon our son. Finally, I would ask if we could come to an agreement without the courts, custody, and attorneys.

"Hello, thanks for calling."

"How is Jamal doing?"

"He is doing good."

There was a moment of awkward silence. "I wanted to talk to you about the divorce petition, specifically the custody."

"What about it?"

I thought, *stay calm and remember what you rehearsed.* "Mark, you're a great father and I wouldn't ever want to keep our son from you. Jamal is only three years old, and he needs his mother."

He interrupted, "And he needs his father too!"

I could see where this was going. I thought, *I'll let him vent a little.*

"Dani, you're always so damn secretive. You think I can trust you? You know, the woman who never even told her parents that we were married. Oh, I forgot, you did... *six months later!*"

"Mark, that's in the past..."

He interrupted me again. "I thought I could make you fall in love with me, but I was wrong. My god, you even refused to take my name!"

I couldn't take it any longer and fell right into his trap. "What about you and all the lies you told? You lied about being married and being legal in this country. Why didn't your wife ever help you get citizenship?"

"Don't you worry about me; we've got enough dirt on you. I will get full custody!"

"Whatever, Mark!" I screamed as I hung up the phone. I thought, *well that didn't go as planned.* After my failed attempt to reason with Mark, I packed and headed to my mother's. I also thought, what did he mean, *we've got enough dirt on you?*

"Hello, Mom. Thanks for picking us up."

"No, problem."

I handed her the baby and loaded our bags. Once Jamal was buckled up, we drove off. I started making small talk to avoid her impending questions.

"Dani, what's going on?"

I thought, *here we go.*

"Mom, it's just like I said, we are getting a divorce."

"A divorce? Why? What is going on?"

"Mom, I don't have much time and I have a lot to do before I leave, so can we table this conversation?"

"When are you leaving?"

"Tomorrow."

"Tomorrow!"

"Yes."

We drove in silence the rest of the way to her house. The rest of my day, I devoted my time to kissing and loving on my son. I tried as best I could to explain to a three-year-old, that Mommy was leaving but would be back soon.

I called every day to check on my baby, sometimes three to four times a day. Everything seemed to be working out, until I received a panicked phone call from my mother.

"Mark came and took Jamal!"

"What?" I screamed "How did you let this happen?"

"He came by and said he wanted to see his son, so I let him in. I didn't know he was going to take him. He walked outside and by the time I turned around he had put Jamal in the car and driven off."

"Did you call the police?"

"No, I'll do it right now!" I thought, *how the hell did she allow this to happen? When did he leave and where has he taken my baby?*

I rushed to work to check all the flights that were departing from Oklahoma City and heading to Los Angeles. I wasn't able to locate my son on any flights out of Oklahoma City. Ugh! Exasperated, I let out a heavy sigh.

"Hello Mom, what did the police say?"

"They said they couldn't do anything, because he is the father and has every right to him, unless there is a court order saying otherwise."

My mother's voice shook. "What did you find out?"

"Not much more, I checked all the flights out of there but didn't find them." "Dani, he was driving a rental car, maybe he drove to a different airport."

"Okay, Mom I've got to go." I thought, *maybe that's it; he drove to another airport and since Dallas was the closest, I'll start my search there.* Bingo! I found him on my first attempt! He was arriving on CO1703. The flight was scheduled to arrive at 8:05 PM.

I waited at the gate with the police officers. As soon as our eyes met, I lunged forward to grab my baby. The officer intervened.

"Is this him?"

"Yes, and that's my baby." The officer handed Jamal to me while the other officer escorted Mark to the opposite side of the boarding area. After taking our statements they privately convened.

"Ma'am, he says he has custody of your son."

"No, that can't be. Yes, we are going through a divorce, but nothing has been settled."

"He has an order giving him temporary custody." The officer showed me the order. I thought, *how could this be? When did he have time to do this?*

"Ma'am, he has also filed a restraining order against you." The officer took my baby out of my arms and handed him to his father. I stood alone and watched him take Jamal away, screaming and crying for me.

Things were moving much faster than I expected and I needed help like yesterday, but I didn't know who I could trust. I thought about asking Arlene McDowell in Human Resources. She wasn't much older than I am, but I always felt wiser at the end of our conversations. At first, I thought *no, it would be too much of an imposition*, but because I was so overwhelmed and in desperate need of assistance, I decided to put my pride aside and reach out to her.

I walked past her office three times before I got the courage to knock on the door. "Hello, Dani."

"Hello, Mrs. McDowell."

"Come on in. And please, call me Arlene."

"Yes, I forgot."

Arlene had heard the rumors that were going around the workplace. She had wanted to reach out to Dani but didn't want to appear too pushy. "What brings you by my office?"

"Uh, well you see…" I thought, *I can't do this. Just turn around and leave.*

"Dani, are you here to talk about what is going on with your son?"

"What do you mean?"

"I think you know what I mean. Dani, I know what happened, so you don't need to give me those details, but if you need help, you need to open up and talk to me."

"Ok."

"Well since that incident, we had an emergency court date, and primary custody was awarded to Mark. I only get to see my son one day a week."

"Oh, my"

"I hired an attorney, but I don't trust her. She didn't even fight for me. The judge ordered me to take a psychology evaluation. I asked her if Mark could be made to take one as well. To this day she hasn't gotten back with me."

"Have you been given the evaluation?"

"Yes. I tried to tell her something was bizarre about the questions the doctor asked."

"What do you mean?"

"The questions didn't have anything to do with my ability to raise children. He just kept asking questions about my father, and our past relationship. He even asked me if I like myself and had I ever thought about harming myself. I guess what I am trying to say is, the inquiry seems to come from a private source."

"Where are you staying now?"

I was too embarrassed to tell her that I was crashing on different friends' couches. So, I stood in silence, hoping she wouldn't push the issue further.

"Dani, I have an extra room. You can move in with me and I know a really good attorney. I'll give him a call."

I was so overjoyed with relief, I burst into tears. "Thank you."

I took a few deep breaths of the smoggy air as I waited for Mark to arrive at the back of the employee parking lot. I hated exchanging Jamal here, but I didn't want to him to know I was semi-homeless. My heart brightened when his car pulled in. I stole a quick glance in the rear-view mirror and tamed my mane of hair.

As I exited my car, I thought, *be polite.* "Hello," I quickly said. I hurried to the passenger rear door and found Jamal slouched over in his seat fast asleep.

"Here, let me help."

"No, no I've got it." I thought, *lord help me; please don't let him get out of this car.* "I've got it! Ok, I'll see you tomorrow."

I didn't comment on anything else, nor did I look at him. I imagined him standing and gloating at my loss of custody, even if it was temporary. I strapped my baby in his car seat and drove off. Fearing that he might follow me to Arlene's house, I took the scenic route to my new home.

Days turned into weeks and weeks into months, and before I knew it a year had passed. I couldn't take seeing Jamal only once a week much longer. I hoped my meeting with my attorney Mr. Lieberman today would bring good news. Mr. Lieberman was an average-looking guy. Most women who measured men by their looks probably wouldn't have given him a second look. But I found him to be a very kind and compassionate man; he reminded me of my stepdad.

For a moment I wondered where he was.

On our first meeting he sat attentively as I divulged my story. I gave him explicit details of the demise of our marriage. I expounded my reasons for taking Jamal to my mother's home. I told him about my mistrust of my last attorney. He chuckled when I said she was taken in by Mark's charms. Finally, I informed him about the psychological evaluation that I was forced to take and how I felt the psychiatrist's questions were unusual and I didn't think they related to the custody battle.

When I asked if we should require Mark to do the same, he suggested that we wait and see what was in the report first. I was devastated, but he assured me this was a typical tactic and not to worry.

A few weeks later I was back in my attorney's office. "Hello Mrs. Baldwin, have a seat. Mr. Lieberman will be right with you."

I gravitated toward the overstuffed Italian leather couch. I picked up a magazine and pretended to read it. The intercom buzzed and moments later I was escorted to his office. As soon as I walked in, Mr. Lieberman stood up.

"Hello Mrs. Baldwin, please take a seat."

I thought, *Lets' get down to business, this meeting is costing me a fortune.* I nervously watched as he fumbled through the papers on his desk.

"Okay, Mrs. Baldwin."

"Dani, please."

"Dani. Well, I have the psychiatrist's report."

I sat up straight and grabbed a hold of the armrest. "In a nutshell, the doctor's report finds you incapable of expressing love and questions your ability to nurture a child. He also suggests you have a profound hatred of men, which seems to stem from your relationship with your father, or lack thereof. He is also concerned that you may have suicidal tendencies."

I closed down. I didn't hear anything else. I wanted to run and hide. *I am going to lose my baby*, is the recording that continued to loop around and around in my mind. When my attorney looked up, he immediately buzzed his secretary to bring water in.

"Mrs. Baldwin," his secretary kept repeating. "Are you ok? Do we need to call a doctor?"

I thought, a doctor for what? "No, I am okay."

I looked at my attorney. "How could he write such things? I was in the psychiatrist's office less than an hour. Not fit to take care of my child?" I didn't realize his secretary was still in the office. "Thank you for the water, I am ok." She looked toward her boss for clearance to leave. He nodded and she left, quietly closing the door behind her.

"Dani, remember I advised you that he will try to discredit you and would go through any length to do so?"

"Yes."

"So, this is his attempt, and this is all circumstantial. They will have to have a lot more than this to prove you're an unfit mother."

"Mr. Lieberman, do you think we should have him evaluated too?"

"Honestly, no I don't, and that move could keep us in court another six to eight months. Is that what you want?"

"No, but I don't want to lose my baby either."

"You won't, but you are going to have to trust me. Now that we know their strategy, I know exactly how to proceed."

Per my attorney's suggestion, we started exchanging Jamal at Arlene's house. I was completely against it, but he suggested it would show stability and my capability to provide a home for Jamal. I was starting to get a little antsy with all of it. I was missing my son dearly and I didn't know how much longer I could ignore Mark's harmful comments. I knew he was just trying to get me riled up, so he could use what I said against me.

At 4:00 PM, Mark pulled up in an old pickup truck. I guessed it belonged to the person he was living with. I gathered Jamal's diaper bag and headed down to turn over my son. Something was different today. Anger from deep within me started to rise. I didn't know if it was the effect of the full moon or that I was at my wits' end. I started to turn around and ask Arlene to deliver Jamal to his dad, but I ignored the thought. I walked proudly over towards Mark. No slumped shoulders today. I stood bravely as he put Jamal in his seat. I thought, *I dare you to say something!*

"Dani, you're never going to win, you're incapable of loving…"

Before he finished his words, I pounced on him like a lioness protecting her cub. I was in a blind rage! So much so, that I didn't notice Arlene's sons were holding me back.

"Get out of here, before she hurts you!"

I could hear whispers of my name being called over and over again. It wasn't until the truck peeled off that I came out of my angry trance.

Once back inside the house, everyone started laughing and giving their narrative of what had happened. I smiled on the outside, but inside I wondered if Jamal witnessed my behavior. I thought for sure I was going to lose custody of my son. I thought, *why didn't I follow my first instincts? I better call my attorney to tell him what happened. But he called before I had a chance.*

"Dani, the phone is for you. It's your attorney," Arlene said.

"Okay, I'll take it in my room."

"Hello Dani, how are you?"

I didn't know what to say.

"Dani?"

"Yes, sorry, I am here."

"I have some good news. We go to court in two weeks!"

When I didn't respond a second time, Mr. Lieberman inquired what was wrong. I told him every detail of what had happened when we exchanged Jamal. "Okay, so how do you feel about exchanging him at the police station?"

"I don't know, ok I guess."

"Dani, don't worry, everything will be ok."

"Will I lose custody?"

"No, and quite frankly, I am glad you finally fought back. Now I have a lot to do. My secretary will call you tomorrow with the details. I think it will be safer to exchange Jamal at the police station. Goodbye Dani."

"Bye," I quietly whispered.

We arrived early to the courthouse; I didn't want to take any chance of running into Mark. My mother and I sat on the hard marble benches outside of the court room. I half-listened as my mother chatted on and on, from one subject to the next. I guess she was just as nervous as I was. When my attorney arrived, I introduced him to my mother. She was going to be his only witness.

"How are you doing Dani?"

"I don't know. I mean…"

As if he knew my next thought, he said "Dani, I need you to fight today, to stand and fight for yourself like you did the other day!" My mother looked baffled.

"I'll explain later Mom."

"It's time to go in," his assistant said. I walked to the front of the courtroom and took the seat next to my attorney. Remembering what he said, I held my head up. I even looked over at Mark. I thought, *you don't scare me…If only I could truly believe it.*

"All rise," the bailiff said.

Mark's attorney was first to present his case. I tried hard to stay focused, just in case they dropped a bomb shell. To my surprise there were no new untruths told, just the grossly fabricated details to his original lies. When his attorney rested his case, my attorney turned to me and asked if me if I had heard anything new. I just shook my head. *No.*

"Dani, everything is going to be just fine."

"Ok," I whispered. I wished I could be as confident as he was.

"Hello, Mr. Okafor, how are you doing today?"

Mark cleared his throat before he answered. "I am doing good."

"How many days after you moved out, did it take you to file for a divorce?"

"I didn't want a divorce…"

"Mr. Okafor, just answer the question. How long did it take you to go and file for a divorce?"

"I don't know. Two, maybe three weeks?"

"Well what was it? Two or three weeks?" My attorney walked over to the table and picked up a piece of paper.

"According to the filing date, it was just a week after you separated. Mr. Okafor, did your wife ever attempt to meet with you and discuss your marriage and Jamal?"

"No."

"Are you sure?" Mark hesitated and looked over to his attorney. I noticed with each question he was asked, his eyes were getting smaller and smaller and shifting back and forth as if he was mesmerized by the hands of a cuckoo clock. A warm, comforting, familiar inner peace invaded my senses. I knew everything was going to be all right. I was startled by the loud rap of the judge's gavel.

I looked at my attorney. I thought, *what is going on? No one moved; it was like time stood still.*

"I am ready to make my ruling on this case. Mr. Lieberman, please take your seat," the judge said.

"Mr. Okafor, you're to return your son immediately to his mother after these proceedings. Furthermore, you will get visitation one day a week. You are ordered to start paying child support immediately." He then looked at Mark's attorney and asked if he had his client's financial records.

"Uh, no, your honor."

"I want those records on my desk by tomorrow morning." The judge then turned toward Mark. "Mr. Okafor, I have never in my career, seen such a futile attempt to discredit another. It is the opinion of the court, that not one word of truth has been uttered out of your mouth today. I am further granting Mrs. Baldwin her car and all of her personal items. The divorce is granted, and the child is to be returned to his mother immediately."

Shortly after the divorce, I moved into a two-bedroom house in Gardenia. I decorated Jamal's room with the 101 Dalmatians. I wanted every day of his life to be filled with bright, loving energy.

"Good night my love," I whispered to my son. I lingered quietly in the shadows, as he tossed and turned in search for the perfect sleeping position. The battle for Jamal's journey home had been exhausting. At times during the divorce proceedings I had lost hope and didn't think this day would ever arrive. I looked towards the heavens and praised God. I took a long, deep breath and one last look at my beloved son before closing his bedroom door.

I thought, *time is the healer of all things*. It had been six months since the divorce and some things had changed for the better. We mutually agreed to co-parent and change some of the stipulations in the custody decree as to visitation. I knew it was a risk to trust Mark but decided it was a risk worth taking for the sake of our son. Besides, the adjustments were working because Jamal was thriving. I set my tea down when I heard the phone ring.

"I'm coming," I said as I ran to pick up the phone.

"Hello," I said.

"It's Mom, calling to check on you and my grandson," she replied.

"Jamal, come and say hello to your Gran-Gran," I instructed. While he spoke with his Gran-Gran, I scurried about preparing a bag for his weekend visit with his father. I could hear him rambling from one subject to another. The doorbell rang and Jamal excitedly screamed "Daddy is here!" and dropped the phone. *Crap*, I thought as I picked up the phone.

"Mom, I'll call you back," and hung up the phone before she could respond.

Before Mark could get fully in the door, Jamal jumped into his father's arms. Looking at the joy on his face, I knew the right decisions had been made. I just hoped my mother would understand.

"His bag is packed and ready," I said.

"Dani, thank you again, I really appreciate you allowing me to be in our son's life," he paused. I could see that he was having an emotional moment.

"I know you do… Jamal, come give Mommy a kiss." I stooped down and he planted a wet kiss on my cheek.

He took a step back. "Mommy, why do you look so sad all the time?"

"I look sad to you?"

"No Mommy, you look sad to the whole world." To emphasize his point he opened his arms wide.

"I'll do better." I fought back my tears.

"Ok, Mommy. I love you."

"I love you more."

"Bye-bye Mommy," he said and out the door they went.

I had rehearsed in my mind over and over again how I was going to tell my mother that we had altered the custody decree. I would take her to her favorite restaurant for lunch. I would insist on her having a few glasses of wine. If she protested, I would gently remind her that she was in good hands with me as her limo driver. She would chuckle and have a second glass of wine. I would patiently wait for the right moment, and then spring it on her. This plot was foolproof; well, it was, at least in my mind.

Fate had decided differently, and it was my own fault. I thought I had plenty of opportunities to tell her about the adjusted custody agreement in a public space. Instead, she found out in a phone call.

"Hello Mom," I nervously said. I hated small talk and hoped to tactfully get the conversation started.

"Was that Mark at the door?" she screeched. There it was; the first jab had been thrown.

I quickly shot back with a resounding "Yes!" and then retreated to my corner and waited for my opponent's next move.

"I thought the court order said you guys were to exchange Jamal at the police station!" she screamed.

I moved the phone away from my ear and continued to listen to her rant.

"After all that man has put you through, you gonna trust him in your home? What did your attorney have to say about all of this?" The tension was almost unbearable. I retreated to my mental corner to explore my options before I threw a counterpunch. My mother continued to belittle me and hurled insults at me.

Her verbal onslaughts attacked my self-worth, self-esteem and had temporary winded me. Once I regained my composure, I replied "We decided that it was in the best interest of our son to discontinue the exchange at the police station." I paused. "I have also agreed to allow Mark see Jamal as much as he wants to!"

"How could you, after all that man has done to you? He tried to destroy you! Have you lost your mind, and who says he won't run away with your baby?"

Before I knew it, we were both standing in the center of the verbal sparring ring, punching and jabbing each other blow-for-blow. All the years of mental abuse seemed to explode in my head, and I became so emotionally charged, I screamed out, "I need you to get the hell out of my business! Mark is a good father and raising Jamal alone was not part of the plan. Unlike you, *I want Jamal to have a relationship with his father!*"

There it was. The knock-out punch, the words I never thought I would say to my mother...All the pent-up rage we had towards each other finally had been put out in the open. We both retreated to our corners. Our hearts were beating so fast and loudly. I could hear the pounding of her heart. I wondered if she could hear mine.

She uttered, "I hope you know what you're doing," and hung up before I could respond.

The next sound I heard was the dial tone. Frustrated, I grabbed my favorite novel off the bookshelf and poured myself a glass of Merlot. I nestled in on the couch, propping pillows all around me. I worked on letting go of the anger and rage I still felt vibrating in my body. After a time, my breathing slowed, and my heart rate balanced. I felt satisfied and safe with the homey space I had created, and I hoped to be able to settle in for a quiet evening.

However, my emotional woes continued to invade my safe haven, making it difficult for me to concentrate on the story. I fought hard to suppress my thoughts, but they were stronger than I. Tears began to flow softly down my cheeks as negative thoughts ran through my mind like a ticker tape. It was all so overwhelming. I set the book down and buried my head into the palms of my hands and cried myself to sleep.

I crawled out of bed still exhausted from yesterday's confrontation with my mom. I had no appetite and decided to go out for a long walk. I gathered my sneakers and sat down to lace them up. I looked up and caught a glimpse of myself in the mirror. I turned away quickly, but my reflection called me back. I couldn't move, I just stared at the image. I thought, *who was this person? I felt certain that this couldn't be me.*

This person did not resemble me at all; her portrayal of me was false. The image reflected a woman without a soul. Her eyes were lifeless and surrounded by dark circles. I moved forward to take a closer look and was astonished how her physical body moved and looked. Her body was slumped over, and she moved like the characters in the movie "The Living Dead."

I stood there in a stupor asking myself, *how did I get here?* I couldn't move; it was like the mirror-me was determined to have my question answered. Then from somewhere deep inside I heard the words *"All you will ever need is inside you!"* I thought, *what the hell does that mean?* I knew I didn't have the strength physically or mentally to deal with my personal issues and still give Jamal the best care possible. My personal struggles would simply have to wait.

I let out a long sigh after hanging up with Mark. I had hoped he could take Jamal to his doctor's appointment. It was always difficult for me to watch the doctors and nurses as they poked and prodded my son. Jamal clutched my hand as we entered the doctor's office.

"Good morning, who do we have here today?" the nurse asked.

I encouraged Jamal to give the nurse his name. "I am Jamal," he said.

"Jamal, what are you here for today?" she asked.

Jamal shrugged his shoulders, "I don't know. Mommy said I have to see the doctor today," he replied.

"We are here to see Dr. Nguyen," I said.

"Mrs. Okafor please take a seat; the nurse will be with you shortly." I held my breath, hoping the nurse didn't say anything about shots. Sensing my nervousness, the nurse gave me one of those reassuring smiles that say *all will be well.*

I began consoling my beloved son, but somehow, I sensed that he knew I was just as scared as he was. I continued to encourage him in spite of my anxiety, and it was working until the door opened and the nursed appeared in a blinding light. Jamal jumped out of his seat and grabbed onto my leg for dear life.

"Jamal Okafor," the nurse called. I stood up to move but Jamal was holding on so tight it made it difficult for me to walk. The nurse stepped forward and took his hand and guided us to a very colorful, kid-friendly examination room.

Jamal immediately let go of the nurse's hand and started to explore the room. This gave the nurse and me time to privately discuss the reason for the visit. The nurse took Jamal's vitals, noted something on his chart, and handed Jamal a sticker for being good. "The doctor will be with you shortly," she said. She placed his chart on the outside of the door and quickly departed.

Doctor Nguyen came bursting into the room a few moments later and gave Jamal a high-five! "So, are you ready to play for the Cowboys?" Dr. Nguyen asked.

"No way, I am going play for my daddy's team, the Rams," Jamal excitedly replied. They both started to laugh.

"Everything looks good, Ms. Baldwin. Any question or concerns?" he asked as he reached for the door handle.

"No," I said.

"Jamal, I'll see you next year, ok buddy?" Dr. Nguyen said as he closed the door behind him.

"Mom, can we go now?" Jamal asked.

I wished I could be as good as Dr Nguyen was in distracting the kids as he performed his check-ups. I could see the uneasiness in Jamal's eyes; it was like he knew something more was to come. I wanted to be courageous and tell him what was coming next, but the truth was I was a cowardly lioness wanting to spare both of us from the vaccination process.

The nurse came in just moments after Dr. Nguyen left. She quickly engaged Jamal into a lively conversation as she gently guided him toward the nurse's station. Suddenly, I heard a child's voice crying out "Dead Man Walking!"

I knew instantly that it was my son. I rushed down the corridor to save him. When I arrived, Jamal was holding onto the doorframe, making a spirited plea for freedom from the inoculation procedure.

I chuckled at the memory, but at the same time I suddenly knew I was a "Dead Woman Walking!" I could no longer run away from the memories. I needed to face my fears. I too must be emotionally vaccinated against my family bloodline, freed of the abusive and emotional neglect. I had to vaccinate pathogens that were causing me dis-ease in my life. More importantly, I innately knew I could no longer put myself on the back burner!

Just when life was beginning to make sense and our family routine had stabilized, I found myself in the midst of a painful self-evaluation. Like an archaeologist, I would need to start the process by a personal excavation. I grabbed my favorite writing pen and journal; it felt good to imagine what thoughts would come forth. I thought, *these blank lines between the binders would soon reveal the source of my pain.*

I turned to the first blank page and dated it…and nothing materialized. My imagination had shut down; even the busy chatter in my mind had ceased. I just sat there staring at the blank pages. I didn't understand what was happening; journaling had always freed me from the outside world. It was how I expressed myself when my vocal chords failed me.

I remembered the situation with Mark and his invasion of my diaries. I couldn't allow the deceptive actions of Mark during our marriage to rob me of my preferred form of self-expression. I had to find a way to forgive him for stealing my childhood diaries and exposing my innermost thoughts to his attorney. Thoughts that were written as a child who was desperate to be loved. A child who longed for a father's love, until her feelings became indifferent towards him.

I was determined to enter a thought, so I patiently waited. Finally, after an eternity, I wrote *The Cultivation of Self.*

The Cultivation of Self? Where did that come? What did it mean? I felt betrayed by my own words, and I set my pen down. I thought, *why would I need to self-examine? It's not* my *fault people are always hurting me. I was looking to blame others for my life; after all wasn't it* them *who had wreaked havoc in my life? They're the reasons why I am in this predicament.* As frightened and disillusioned as I was upon writing this, I knew those words held the truth to my healing. I thought, *where do I start?*

Suddenly, I felt a gentle breath rising inside me and heard the words, *everything you will ever need is inside, Wondering Butterfly.* At that moment, I knew my great-Grandma Maikoda was guiding me.

I thought out loud, *Grandma Maikoda, I don't know exactly what I am to do.* I sat, still waiting for an answer. Unconsciously, I reached for my journal and this time my thoughts flowed onto the blank pages. I remember the long run I took years ago in Hawai'i. I could still smell the sweet fragrances of the flowers and feel the sunshine kissing my skin as I wrote. I stopped mid-sentence, and thought, *God is still with me and I am loved. Is this what you mean Grandma, God is with me and still loves me?*

The words poured feverishly onto the pages. I filled page after page of my journal. I was a willing participant.

I became like a cocooned butterfly. I shut out everyone and sojourned inwardly. I knew for some of the people in my life, the separation would be temporary, but for others it would be the end of our journey.

In mining my soul, I discovered destructive patterns and behaviors that repeatedly appeared. Abandonment, rejection, low self-esteem, and lack of self-love were the immediate emotions that presented themselves in my writings. I started to examine the people in my life, in particular the women. I examined my mother's life as it related to me.

I found that I felt abandoned by her both emotionally and physically. *My god*, I thought, *she was not able to tell me she loved me until I was twenty-years old!* I couldn't recall a single gentle moment where she expressed emotions with a touch of love of any kind. How did she get to where she couldn't show her own child love?

Next, I thought of my Grandmother Eva. I searched and searched my memory for acts of love between her and my mother. I couldn't recall one. Not even during all of visits when we lived abroad was love ever demonstrated between them. I think my mother was trying to buy her love with those trips aboard. I too did the same with my mother; I would buy her elaborate gifts to win her approval. I thought of all stories Grandma Eva shared about her mother Eula; not one of them revealed any act of love. There were plenty of stories of shame and abuse and unjust acts to cover them up.

Many years later when I revealed to my mother my sexual abuse and the abuser, her uninterested response was, *yeah that happened to me too.* I was confused with her response. Was it acceptable that my innocence was stolen in such a way? At first, I was angry with her, then I realized, *I can't look to others to help me with my healing process, not even my mother. This is a path that I must walk alone.* I thought maybe the women in my life did only what they knew to do survive.

Meditation and journaling brought a great deal of peace in my life, but sadness and shame permeated the shadows of my life. I desired relief from this battle within. I decided to attack the behaviors that were controlling my life. One positive step forward was to join a group of survivors.

I was nervous about sharing my shameful past of molestation and rape. Although everyone within my group had similar experiences, somehow I believed that I deserved what had happened to me. While resting in my stillness, I started to question who I was. In some parts of my life I showed tremendous strength and courage, whereas in other areas my behaviors were child-like.

One day, during an exercise in my therapy group for sexually abused individuals, I met her, my inner child. She was spirited and rambunctious. I liked her instantaneously. Although she was part of me, I felt separate from her. I drew a picture of her peeking out at me. I burst out laughing. The therapist looked my way. *I just met her!* I thought. *I do have a voice. All I need is within me, just like Grandma Maikoda had said.*

Going inside is the first step to taking back my life. I learned about myself through her. Her boisterousness served me, as did my quietness. I remember when a group of girls attacked me after school one day. *I was getting off the bus and they encircled me. Calling me names and telling me what they were going to do to me. I said nothing. I wasn't even scared. My mother's words were in the forefront of my mind. "You don't ever start a fight, but if someone attacks you; fight back." One of the girls knocked my books out of my hand, and I gained the strength of a hundred. When my mother arrived at the bus stop, they were all on the ground nursing their wounds. I don't remember what happened, but I do remember my mother gently shaking me to bring back to the present.*

I never had any more problems in school after that.

I now understand that my inner child had protected me for all these years. She was the one who helped me survive the rape and molestation. She kept all those painful memories away until I was ready to deal with them.

I excelled in my therapy group; soon I became an open book within the group. I found that every time I talked about my experiences, they had less power over me.

Through my inner child I was learning self-acceptance. I could no longer accept others' opinions of me as truth. One day as I was applying lipstick before heading out to run errands, I noticed I avoided eye contact with myself. I tried again to look at myself and did the same thing. I thought, *what is going on? Why can't I look at myself? Not now Dani,* I said to myself, *you got things to do.* I grabbed my purse and took off. During my day, I noticed that I rarely made direct eye contact with others; I always seemed to divert my eyes in another direction when in conversation or passing others.

Later that evening I poured myself a nice merlot and sat directly in front of my full-length mirror. I started scanning my body from the bottom up. I did pretty well on the lower half but as my eyes grew nearer to my face, I became tense. I tried a few more times and failed. I thought, *admit it Dani, you just don't like yourself. How did I get here?* It was evident that I didn't love myself. I couldn't recall as a child ever hearing the words *I love you*. I thought, *I have work to do. I will have to dig deeper.* I wondered if I had the strength.

Over time I learned that the best thing to do, and the hardest thing to do, was to learn to forgive. To forgive those who wronged me, as well as myself for being too small to defend myself. It was the first step in the healing process. The process Is on-going, but every step I take on the healing path Is easier and easier.

In Conclusion

Forgiveness

Forgiveness is the ability to heal past grievances. It is the power to release someone of a perceived wrongdoing. True forgiveness doesn't rest in telling someone that you forgive them in one breath and in the next breath tell them that you will never forget. Is that true forgiveness? No, it is not. Although I felt some temporary relief as I forgave people, sustainable tranquility eluded me. I still had bitterness and anger raging inside of me.

I learned true forgiveness came when I was able to fully release the incident(s) from the level of causation. Getting to the heart of the pain is the first step. Being willing remove the blinders and truly see. It took me many years to heal the fragile relationship with my mother.

Even if my mother had come to me and apologized, I wouldn't have truly forgiven her at first. The wounds were so deep, that a simple band aid would not have sufficed. It would give me temporary release from the pain, but soon the pus would surface and the band aid would fall off, exposing my wounds.

I needed to be absolutely clear about what I was healing, and understanding the source of my pain. If, I truly wanted to heal.

The journey I embarked on through journaling, meetings, and counseling, took back four generation of mental and physical abuse. Next, I had to give it a name, expose the wounds, call them out!

Mental and physical abuse. Self-hate and unworthiness. How do you unsee physical abuse? How do you heal the deep longing to be loved an accepted? How do you erase years of self-sabotaging behaviors? How do you admit all you ever wanted was to hear those three words, *I love you*?

I found I had more questions than answers. The journey ahead seems to be an impossible undertaking. I started and quit so many times, until I learned it was ok for me to be angry and express anger, sadness, disappointment, and loneliness. That it was important to *feel* each step of this journey.

This made the process a little easier for me to continue. Oddly enough, the forgiveness of my father was easier, perhaps because he chose not to be involved in my life, and there was not real attachment.

The forgiveness of my mother would take several seasons. I can remember the exact moment when it happened. It was when I understood that I must forgive myself first.

The healing I was searching for was not as much about me forgiving her as it was about me forgiving me!

Once I had done as much healing as I could surrounding my mother and our relationship, I realized that in order to complete my healing, I needed to not only forgive her, but I needed to forgive myself.

I needed to forgive myself for being small and defenseless, forgive myself for putting up defense mechanisms that served me in childhood but burdened me in adulthood, and forgive myself for hurting. I realized that the healing I was searching for would only be complete when I learned to forgive myself, and let myself open up to people, love, and happiness.

I needed to let the child inside of me know I was proud of her, that I loved her, and I didn't blame her for anything that happened to her. Rather, I was proud of her for defending me when I was small, but it was time for me to love her back.

In my personal experience, when I have sojourned inward and took responsibility for what has shown up in my life, I experienced true peace. Does this mean I am responsible for the person who molested me? Or my mother's treatment of me? Of course not!

But as an adult I am responsible for seeking assistance for my anger and pain, and for seeking help when needed. Over time and much journaling and therapy sessions, I was able to completely forgive the person for the violent act against me. This allowed me to take back all my power! Simply put, in order to experience complete healing(s), we must be willing to forgive fully.

Just as one can imagine life's reflections in the clouds, I in my moments of happiness saw unlimited possibilities in myself. Inside my heart I heard, *all has not been wasted my child, your path is unique and magical; serve the Universe well and the Universe will serve you.*

About the Author

Yolanda Bradford was born in Oklahoma City, Oklahoma. Growing up, she was consumed with what was beyond the red dirt of her home state. At a young age her mother married a military man and they were whisked away from the humdrum life of Oklahoma City to new and exciting places. Although she escaped her birthplace, her battle  to self-love had just begun. Yolanda created and teaches the 7 butterfly principles, a practical guide to self-healing. Yolanda's first published story "Finishing the Dance" can be found in *Pebbles in the Pond* 4th edition.